PAINFUL CONSEQUENCES

by

ALISON NORTH

I0457521

Book One - Jennie and Friends
Chapter One - The School Secretary's Tale of Woe
Prologue

As she bent right forward across the mahogany writing table, red-faced and very bare bottomed, she could recall the incident well. 'Hello, gorgeous!' that cheeky Jonathan Crowe had cried, having answered the doorbell almost immediately. 'So you've decided to take up my offer at last?'

'Hello, Jonathan,' she'd replied. 'Exactly which offer is that?'

'The offer of my services, of course. The same offer I make every time I get a chance to have a word with you on your own. The one you very nearly accepted in Majorca last January.'

'Oh, that offer? No, I'm afraid I've just brought you a file from Michael. He'd like you to read it and then give him a ring later.'

'How disappointing. But will you come in for a while?'

'Yes please. Michael wants me to take a couple of the drawings back to him tonight, actually.'

'Fine. Help yourself to a sherry while I make a start. Christopher's there in the living room. We were just having a drink and a chat before he sets off for London.'

'Hi, Chris,' she called as she walked into the room. 'How's every little thing?'

'There's no need to talk about Christopher's private parts like that,' Jonathan quipped at once.

'Jonathan!' she choked with laughter, trying not to blush.

'I like your kit,' he grinned, closely eyeing the seat of her tiny white sports skirt in the wall mirror behind her, before unashamedly transferring his gaze to the tightly fitting top. 'Squash, is it?'

'No, badminton actually.'

'Anyway, make yourself at home. Remove whatever items of clothing are uncomfortable, please do.'

So she poured herself a drink and sat down. Jonathan had started reading the file of papers, but every now and then he directed some outrageously raunchy remark towards her. Just as he always did, even when Michael was there.

'Here you are, then,' he said, some thirty minutes later. 'Those are the drawings Michael wants back tonight. Now you can go home and cook him a lovely dinner, and then enjoy an evening of wedded bliss. After your badminton, of course.'

'Oh, I shan't be doing that. After the badminton class I'm off for a drink or three with Alison and the rest of the girls. Mike's dinner's in a tin somewhere, I expect.'

'What?' Jonathan gasped with mock dismay. 'His dinner's in a tin?'

'Too right. I've told him I'm going to enjoy myself. I'm not getting involved with cooking tonight. He can look after himself.'

'If you were my wife and said that to me after a hard day's work, I'd put you over my knee and spank you.'

'Oh no you wouldn't,' she laughed.

'Oh yes I would,' he growled.

'It would take a man, not a shirt-button,' she goaded rudely, poking out her tongue for good measure.

'A shirt-button?'

'Yes, a shirt-button.'

'I see,' Jonathan murmured, taking a step in her direction. 'I'm a shirt-button, am I?'

'Yes, you are.'

'I'm a shirt-button, and if I were your husband my dinner would be somewhere in a tin?'

'That's right,' she giggled.

'So, let's get this straight. I'm your husband, let's say. I'm your husband, I'm a shirt-button, and my dinner's somewhere in some tin?'

'Absolutely correct.'

'And I'm not about to put you over my knee, I suppose?'

'No, you're not, *shirt-button*.'

'Well, we'll see about that.' Suddenly, and rather skilfully, he caught her by the wrist and tugged her to her feet.

'Hey, let go!' she squealed in surprise, almost spilling her sherry.

'Not until you apologise.'

'I'd be careful if I were you,' Christopher warned her, with a large grin. 'Jonathan can be rather impetuous, you know.'

'Oh, can he really?' she retorted defiantly, placing her glass on the coffee table.

'Apologise,' Jonathan repeated.

'I never apologise to a shirt-button,' she'd been unable to stop herself saying, before sticking out her tongue once again.

'That does it! This particular shirt-button is going to drag you over to that chair, sit down, pull you over his knee, and then he's going to wallop your fat little bottom with all his force.'

'He isn't.'

'He is.'

'Oh, no he's not.'

'Oh, yes he is.'

'He certainly isn't,' she gasped, suddenly alarmed and trying unsuccessfully to free her wrist from his hold. 'He most certainly is not!'

But, unfortunately for her, she was wrong. He most certainly was going to do it... and did. Despite her shrieks of protest and her struggles to escape, the sound of a hard male hand impacting noisily on soft, bare buttocks started to echo right through the house. And continued to echo. But after only a minute or so her protests and struggles ceased, leaving her lying submissively over Jonathan's knee, tearfully accepting her fate, while at the same time becoming wetter and wetter at the junction of her thighs. She hadn't even raised an objection when

Jonathan eventually invited Christopher, who was conveniently left-handed, to lay a few heavy smacks on her himself. Thereafter the spanking proceeded in turns - a dozen from Jonathan on each cheek, followed by the same from Christopher, then Jonathan again, then Christopher once more, until she completely lost track of whose hand was whose...

And the rest of it was just history now. Including the highly unsavoury use to which Jonathan's four-seater settee had been put once the men were satisfied that her poor, grossly over-exposed posterior was painted a suitably chastened hue...

Part One

Mr Stanley sat back in his comfortable swivel armchair and pushed the short typewritten report towards the centre of the desk. For at least the tenth time that morning he called to mind the image that had haunted him throughout the past eighteen months - a very short, very smart business skirt, dark blue, black, or grey. A very short, very smart business skirt, the seat of which was always stretched so exquisitely across the spectacular swell of the shapeliest pair of buttocks it had ever been his privilege to behold. Not that 'privilege' had always been the right word, he thought to himself with a sardonic smile. Not until today. Previously 'torment' would have been much more appropriate. But all that was now about to change...

And looking up from the skirt - which he only ever did with reluctance - there would be the invariable crisp white blouse, nipped in tightly betwixt bust and waist, and overlapping the top of her skirt by no more than half an inch...

He reached for the red intercom button that connected his room to the small adjoining office of the school secretary. 'Mrs Jamieson,' he said with quiet authority. 'I wonder if you could come through here for a while.'

Which colour skirt would it be today? Blue, black, or grey? He rather hoped it would be his favourite. The dark blue one that had made its first appearance last February. It would be most appropriate if she were to wear it today of all days. 'Come in,' he called in response to the almost immediate tap on the door.

'Good morning, Headmaster,' she said brightly, leaving the sliding door that connected the two rooms wide open - as well as the large sash window in her own room. An oversight she was to regret bitterly before the day was through.

'Would you be good enough to turn on the air conditioning?' he said, his eyes glued with their usual intensity to the lateral swing of deliciously bouncy buttocks as they undulated gracefully across the room. Buttocks so pert and perfect that the merest glimpse had been known to make grown men break down and weep openly in the street.

It was his favourite, he noted with more than a twinge of satisfaction. The blue one that had first been worn last Valentine's Day. The one that had tortured him more than any other. Excellent! Truly excellent! Yes, it was most appropriate that she should be wearing it today! It was noticeably shorter and tighter than the rest. And made from such thin, lightweight material that it clung delightfully to the cheekiest part of her lovely bottom, displaying it to perfection.

He stared with fascination at the merest hint of panty-line on show. It ran, very briefly, in diagonals across the centre of each pouting cheek. As in the past, he speculated with interest on the colour of the knickers. Did they match her skirt, in the same way that her high heels always did? Or were they, perhaps, a riotous multitude of colours, or maybe snowy-white and innocent? Or were they black and very naughty? Of one thing he could be sure; they were just as small and skimpy as it was possible for them to be. The outline through her skirt assured him of that.

'And would you be kind enough to file these documents in the sixth form filing cabinet?' he continued smoothly, thereby granting himself at least another sixty seconds during which he could ogle her mouth-wateringly plump rear end. This was standard procedure, but today the only emotion he felt was one of pure elation. Of frustration, there was none.

'Is there anything else, sir?' she asked, standing there in front of his desk - tall, blonde, and stunningly attractive as she smiled politely at him.

'Yes, I'm afraid there is,' he replied, seeing the smile fade from her face at the unexpected frostiness of his response. 'I think you should read this report from our Deputy Headmistress. Perhaps you can guess what it concerns?'

'Oh dear...'

'Others may make light of this sort of situation, but I should tell you here and now that I take a very serious view of it. A very serious view indeed.'

'But, Mr Stanley...'

'Please be so good as to read the report, Mrs Jamieson.'

Knowing what it would be about, Jennie felt herself going red in the face as she picked up the two typewritten pages and started to read...

Internal Communication from the Deputy Headmistress, Miss Amelia Stricton, to the Headmaster, Mr Stanley.

Headmaster, I feel it my very clear duty to inform you of an incident that occurred on school premises last night during the cocktail party for the new school governors.

At about 9.15 p.m. I left the staffroom to make a private telephone call from my office. On passing the chemistry lab I noticed the room was partially illuminated. On closer inspection I detected voices within and decided I had to investigate.

I opened the door quietly and noted that two people were present: Mrs Jamieson (school secretary) and Mr Parker (sports master).

Mrs Jamieson was bent across one of the lab benches, her toes only just touching the floor. Her dress was unzipped at the back and raised. Her bra was dangling from a nearby Bunsen burner.

She was totally devoid of any other clothing, apart from her high-heeled shoes and an inadequate pair of knickers around one ankle.

Mr Parker was standing directly behind her wearing only a T-shirt and a pair of gym shoes. His shorts had been discarded on the floor, and the couple were fornicating.

I decided it only appropriate to make my presence known, so I entered and slammed the door behind me. The result on Mr Parker was instantaneous, for he let out a strangled expletive and shuffled backwards two or three feet, his embarrassing physical condition confirming that they were indeed indulging in physical union.

There followed a delay of some thirty seconds or so, for reasons I'd prefer not to elaborate upon in this report. During this unseemly interval it became apparent that my presence remained undetected by Mrs Jamieson, for she continued to moan and move in a highly lascivious manner. Eventually I had to tap her on the shoulder and tell her to stand up.

Thereafter I asked both for an explanation, but none was forthcoming. I therefore ordered them to replace their clothing and return to the staffroom, and for the remainder of the function I kept both in sight to ensure no repetition of this most unsavoury episode.

A. Stricton, Deputy Headmistress, Longfields Private Boarding School for the Children of Her Majesty's Officers of the Armed Forces.

Having finished the report, Jennie stared unseeingly at the last few lines of type. Well at least there was one consolation, she told herself with a sigh; the report made no detailed mention of the embarrassing way in which last night's episode had ended. It was all Miss Stricton's fault, of course. Her sense of timing had been absolutely appalling. She'd banged the door shut at precisely the wrong moment; at precisely the moment that Mr Parker was getting it all together. She banged the door shut, and as she said in her report, Mr Parker leapt back in alarm. He leapt backwards all of a sudden as if he'd just been shot. He leapt off her back. He leapt off her back and then... and then... and then he shot his lot! All over her! Great, thick globules of hot spunk started to splatter and splash in a sudden torrent all over the upturned cheeks of her bottom. She'd never known such a cascade. It gushed forth unabated for what seemed ages. Unfortunately, she herself had been far too preoccupied with her own orgasm to hear the door bang shut or realise that anything was wrong. She just continued to lie there, squirming her bottom from side to side and wondering why Mr Parker had decided to finish off in that slightly unusual way. Eventually something made her glance over her shoulder and she'd been horrified to see Miss Stricton right at her side, her face a picture of mingled rage and disgust.

How uncomfortable it had been for the rest of the evening. How uncomfortable, standing in the staffroom for the next two hours with the soaking wet seat of her short, tight cocktail dress pressed out of sight against the wall. And how embarrassing it had been trying to carry on a polite conversation with the chaplain and the new chairman of the governors whilst all the time able to feel sticky dollops of Mr Parker dribbling slowly but surely down the deep cleft between her cheeks.

Fortunately Michael was fast asleep by the time she got home, so there'd been no additional complications there, although he partially roused for his nightly slice of nooky the second she slid into bed beside him. Utilising his standard 'back-scuttle' technique, of course. Why did everyone want to do it to her that way? From behind, instead of in front? It had been the same ever since the age of fifteen, so she'd spent the last thirteen years of her life being made love to behind her back. Why was that? Was it just because her bottom was quite a nice shape...?

Now what was it that Mr Parker said to her at the party last night? Before the catastrophe in the chemistry lab. What was it he said as he stood beside her in the corner of the staffroom, furtively fondling every inch of her bottom through her smart new cocktail dress? Oh, yes of course, that was it. He whispered into her ear that she'd got the prettiest, peachiest little arse he'd ever laid eyes or hands on. And that if he didn't get to mount it some day soon he'd burst a blood vessel - as well as a zip. She'd giggled and taken another gulp of her gin and tonic, and then told him that it was almost too much of a responsibility for her to bear. Five minutes later they'd been at it like knives in the chemistry lab... Fido-fashion, needless to say.

'Surely you've read it by now?' Mr Stanley asked sharply, drumming his fingers on the top of the desk as he sat there, formally dressed in black mortarboard and gown.

'Er, yes sir, I've just finished...'

'Well?'

'Oh, um, er...'

'Well, is it true?' he snapped. 'Is Miss Stricton's report an accurate account of what happened last night?'

'Yes, sir.'

'You don't deny the allegations against you?'

'No, sir.'

'I see. You realise the gravity of this matter?'

'I had been drinking, sir.'

'I don't want to hear any feeble excuses,' he insisted. 'That will just make matters worse. My only concern is that you have just admitted a very serious breach of trust.'

'I'm sorry...'

'Being sorry is hardly enough,' he said icily. 'This is an educational establishment, and the children in this establishment are placed here in my trust and under my care and protection.'

'Yes, sir.'

'I have a duty. A bounden duty. I have a duty to ensure that the trust vested in me is not misplaced. To this end, discipline has to be maintained.'

'Yes, sir.'

'I am obliged to see that the children are set an example. An exemplary example. I owe the parents of those children a duty to enforce a proper code of moral conduct. Not only on the children themselves, but also on my staff. How else can the children be guided in the right direction except by the precept and example of the staff? And the staff includes the school secretary, does it not, Mrs Jamieson?'

'Yes, sir.'

'If I can't rely on my staff to set the right example, then I might as well give up and go home. I would rather stand in the dole queue than breach the sacred trust that has been placed in me by the guardians of those innocent young people. To my mind this is a matter of the utmost gravity, and one for which a suitable punishment has to be imposed.'

'Yes, sir. I'm really very sorry.'

'As I said, that is not enough. The damage has already been done. And I think you'll agree that it can scarcely be reversed?'

'Not really...'

'I shall have to make an example of you. An example that will deter others beyond any shadow of a doubt.'

'Yes, sir.'

'So I have reached a very painful decision.'

'Yes, sir?'

'Your contract of employment will be terminated forthwith. You will be dismissed without notice, and without pay in lieu of notice.'

'Yes, sir.'

'You will be dismissed on the grounds of your gross misconduct and dire dereliction of duty.'

'Yes, sir,' she sighed, having already resigned herself to that particular fate in view of his attitude so far. Well, it wasn't the end of the world. This part-time job was only an interest. They didn't need the money, after all. Michael earned more than enough to enable them to live life to the full. She'd just have to tell him she'd gotten bored with the job and resigned...

'And I shall personally ensure that Mr Jamieson is informed of the reasons for your dismissal. The exact reasons for your dismissal.'

'Oh no!' she squealed in horror. 'You can't do that!'

'I certainly can, young lady. In fact, I shall hand him a copy of Miss Stricton's report myself, so there can be no shred of doubt as to why you've been summarily dismissed.'

'No, no, you can't! You mustn't!'

'I can, I must, and I will. This very afternoon.'

'Oh no, Mr Stanley. I beg you not to do it. It would be the end of me.'

'You should have thought of that earlier, Mrs Jamieson. Before you set forth to copulate on school premises, during a formal school function, and with another member of school staff.'

'But he'll kill me! He'll never forgive and forget. Not after what happened last year—'

'I'm afraid that's no concern of mine. I'm here to uphold the moral discipline of this establishment, and to make absolutely certain that the young persons in my care and control are not subjected to invidious outside influences.'

'But you can sack me without telling my husband why.'

'As I've said already, an example has to be made. Mere dismissal from your post would be totally inadequate. Justice must be seen to be done. And it follows, inexorably, that the punishment must be made to fit the crime.'

'But there must be an alternative,' she pleaded desperately. 'There must be another way. Surely my husband doesn't have to be involved?'

'I can't think of any alternative course of action.'

'I'm sure there must be one, Mr Stanley.'

'If there is, it eludes me completely.'

'There must be another option, Headmaster? Surely there must? You can think of one if you try.'

'I really don't know that I can.'

'Please think, Mr Stanley, *think*.'

'I am thinking, Mrs Jamieson. Very hard indeed.'

'And?'

'And I'm totally bereft of ideas.'

'But you can't be.'

'But I am.'

'What, totally bereft?'

'Yes, totally.'

'Surely not, Mr Stanley?'

'I'm afraid I am.'

'Oh, Mr Stanley,' she wailed, hopping from one foot to the other in anguish and despair. 'Please, please think of something. It's a matter of life and death. Please, please think of something else.'

'I suppose... there is one other solution...' he said slowly, after a much longer pause for thought. 'Although I'm not totally convinced that it's altogether suitable.'

'Of course it is, Headmaster. I'm certain it must be.'

'And also, I doubt whether you'd find it substantially more palatable than my original plan.'

'I will, Mr Stanley, I will. I can assure you one hundred percent of that fact.'

'Can you really?' he murmured, a sardonic smile returning to his lips. 'I really wonder whether you can.'

'Yes, yes, Mr Stanley. Anything will be better than telling my husband about last night.'

'I wonder whether you'll feel the same by the end of the morning,' he mused, sitting back in his comfortable chair and allowing the smile to broaden.

Jennie was hardly listening. She was too delighted with herself. Phew! It had been a close run thing, but it seemed clear that the danger had passed. It had been far too close for comfort, but somehow she'd managed to talk him round. And now he was much more relaxed about the whole unfortunate affair...

'You haven't yet enquired as to the nature of the alternative,' he pointed out, almost pleasantly. 'Or perhaps you've guessed already?'

'Not really, Headmaster.'

'Are you sure?'

'Yes, Headmaster.'

'Your lack of imagination surprises me, Mrs Jamieson. After all, this is a school, is it not? A private fee paying school, to be accurate. And is there not one type of punishment that is particularly prevalent - indeed, one might even say traditional - in such an establishment?'

'Is there, Mr Stanley?' she enquired, somewhat bemused.

'Come, come, Mrs Jamieson. Do I really have to remind you what it is?'

'I'm afraid you do.'

'I'm amazed. I'd have thought the answer would be staring you in the face.' He smiled to himself, rather thinly. 'Or perhaps that's not quite the way to put it. But never mind. You really need me to spell it out for you, Mrs Jamieson?'

'Yes, sir, if you don't mind too much.'

'Really and truly? You can't even hazard a guess?'

'No, sir...'

'You want me to explain in detail exactly what it is that you'll be so happy for me to do to you?'

'Yes please, sir. I genuinely don't have a clue.'

'Then allow me to give you one,' he murmured coolly, reaching into a cupboard by his side. 'A rather obvious one, I'm afraid.'

'Thank you, sir.'

'Here it is,' he said, placing a long thin cane on the desktop immediately in front of her. It was bound with black leather and had a looped handle of the same material. 'Now perhaps you understand?'

She stared in surprise at the evil-looking instrument of torture that reminded her of a grossly oversized horsewhip. 'What on earth are you going to do with that?' she asked at length, completely bewildered.

He stared icily into her eyes. 'Come now, Mrs Jamieson,' he replied with a distinctly cruel edge to his voice. 'What do you think I'm going to do with it?'

She felt her mouth and throat going dry at the thought of what he meant. She looked down at the cane once again, her stomach starting to churn with a mixture of horror and cold fear. 'But the cane is for children,' she only just managed to gasp. 'I'm a married woman, with children of my own...'

He flexed the cane in his hands. It was strong and surprisingly weighty, yet sufficiently whippy as well. 'Fear not, Mrs Jamieson,' he murmured, 'I'm quite sure that this particularly splendid specimen is more than capable of dealing with you effectively. Very effectively indeed. You needn't concern yourself about that. You have my word on it. The word of an officer and a gentleman, as well as a doctor of letters. Rest assured, you have nothing to worry about on that score. Nothing at all. The cane will do its duty towards you, married woman or not. Believe me, please. I promise - most sincerely.'

Jennie took a nervous step back, at the same time staring wide-eyed at the fiendish implement of cruelty that once again lay, so menacingly, on the desk before her. She could see for herself how easily it would cut right down into the fleshy cheeks of her bottom. 'You can't really be intending to use that thing on me?' she croaked, unable to believe her eyes and ears.

'I certainly didn't intend to,' he lied smoothly. 'I intended to dismiss you and inform your good husband of the reason for such dismissal. If you remember correctly, you were the one who pleaded for an alternative course of action. It's entirely up to you. If you prefer I'll implement my original plan of action without further delay. I'll phone your husband for an appointment right now, if that's what you'd prefer me to do. The choice is entirely yours.'

'I must be dreaming,' she groaned, taking another step away from the desk. 'There's simply no other explanation. This is nothing but a bad dream.'

'Believe it if you like, but that cane looks very real to me. Perhaps you'd care to put your theory to the test? Perhaps you'd care to turn your back on me and count to ten? By that time I can promise you'll have the answer. Oh yes, the answer will be very clear indeed. Painfully clear, I should say.'

Jennie could still not believe her senses. 'You really mean to say that you'll tell my husband about last night unless I let you cane me?'

'That's precisely so, Mrs Jamieson. You have summed it up most succinctly. I couldn't have put it better myself. Heartfelt congratulations.'

'But it just isn't right...'

'Lot's of things in this world aren't right. Last night is a prime example. Was it right for you to grant Mr Parker carnal knowledge of yourself, bottoms-up across a laboratory bench?'

'No, it wasn't the right thing to do. But on the other hand it wasn't the worst thing in the world either.'

'Quite correct, young lady. And there are also worse things in the world that could happen to you other than having your bottom set alight by this particularly well wrought cane. Not many, perhaps, but some. Like separation and divorce, for instance. And protracted court battles over the custody of your children and the distribution of the matrimonial assets.'

'I suppose I don't have any choice?' she muttered, still scarcely able to believe the situation.

'Oh, but you do. The choice is very clear. The sack and a copy of this report to your husband, or continuity of employment and marital harmony at the cost of an exceptionally thorough caning across those grossly adulterous cheeks.' As he spoke he glanced momentarily at their proud, lightly clad reflection in the glass-fronted bookcase behind her. Then he continued. 'Twelve of the very, very best, laid across them with all the strength I can muster. Sufficient to set them on fire for a week!'

'It's all so terribly unfair.'

'I'm not convinced that your good husband would agree with you there. Not if he were fully conversant with all the relevant facts of the case. I think he might lend his support - nay, even his encouragement - to what I have to do. What are your views on that, Mrs Jamieson? I shall be interested to hear.'

She made no reply. Slowly she shook her head, utterly bewildered and

11

bemused. What more could she say to this man? It seemed that it really was going to happen to her - twelve really hard strokes of the cane across her poor bottom! She supposed she should try to get used to the idea...

'So then, young lady, decision time. Which shall it be? My first and original plan, or the alternative choice that you begged me to offer you? The alternative, may I remind you, that you assured me you'd find more acceptable.'

She dropped her gaze to the carpet. 'You know which one it has to be,' she whispered.

Mr Stanley was so elated he had to warn himself not to let it show. He had good reason to be pleased, of course. This was, after all, the realisation of a lifelong fantasy. A fantasy given physical form some eighteen months earlier when she'd first started to work for him. Of course, he'd never expected the fantasy to be fulfilled. Never in a million years. Yet the yearning for fulfilment had at times driven him to the brink. Every glimpse of those saucy cheeks snaking from side to side as she walked had been torture of the very worst kind. Every glimpse of those pert cheeks hidden away under cover of a short, snug-fitting business skirt had driven him to distraction and beyond...

And now, here he was, on the verge of achieving that which he'd hitherto deemed impossible. So he'd take his time and enjoy himself to the full.

'A very wise decision,' he replied, after a wait of at least a minute. 'My congratulations to you.'

Jennie didn't answer. She stood in front of him with her head bowed, blushing with embarrassment as she waited to see how he intended to proceed.

'So I suppose we'd better get started on this rather distasteful business,' he sighed. 'You're aware of what's expected of you, I presume?'

'Well, not exactly...'

'But you do have a broad general outline?'

'Yes, I've got that much, I'm extremely sorry to say.'

He smiled without warmth. 'If it's any consolation, you'll be a great deal sorrier before you leave this room. A very great deal sorrier.'

'Oh,' she sniffed forlornly, blinking as she felt herself starting to cry.

'I'm afraid this is not the time for tears, Mrs Jamieson. Although I can assure you that there'll be no shortage of them later. Very much the opposite, in fact. Now then, this is what I want you to do...'

Mr Stanley continued to lounge back in the luxury of his swivel armchair. With quiet authority he explained exactly what was required. First he drew her attention to a mahogany writing table that stood in the corner of the alcove of a huge bay window, in front of and a few feet to the right of his desk. A tall wooden chair had been pushed right up to the table, the back of which towered some ten inches above the writing surface.

She was then instructed to stand directly behind the chair, facing the table. In this way her back, bathed in filtered sunlight from the window, was turned approximately three-quarters towards the spot where Mr Stanley sat watching.

He was taking his time, as he'd earlier promised himself he would. This was just too good to rush, he gloated to himself. And anyway, the longer he made her wait the more her anxiety would grow. Already she was visibly unnerved, as witness the occasional twitch of each pouting buttock while she stood with her hands gripping the top of the chair. He'd study those involuntary movements for a few minutes longer, before issuing further orders. He felt confident they'd become ever more pronounced as time ticked slowly by. Mind you, her present agitation was as nothing compared to what she had in store. Those juicy-ripe cheeks at which he was staring would be trembling even more before the cane began to rise and fall. But that was far in the future. There was a great deal of procedure to undergo before the first excruciating cut...

Mr Stanley's next set of instructions was very precise indeed. It was precise because the instructions were immensely important. Calmly but firmly she was told she had to bend forward over the top of the chair. All the way forward, until her forehead and forearms were resting on the writing table beyond and below. He wanted 'that ruttish little rear end' - he informed her - pointing at the window and several inches above the level of her head. He wanted it to be the highest part of her person above the floor. No compromise would be tolerated.

After he'd finished speaking there was a noticeable hesitation on her part, and it seemed possible she might rebel. At length he spoke again. 'Bend over, Mrs Jamieson,' he said bleakly, confident that eventually she would comply. 'Bend over, just as I ordered.'

She darted a furtive look back at him as he sat at his desk, grim-faced and with the hellish-looking cane held purposefully in his right hand.

'Bend over,' he repeated as frostily as before. She opened her mouth to protest, but then thought better of it.

'Bend over,' he said yet again, tightening his grip on the cane as he spoke.

She stared down at the highly polished tabletop, groaning miserably to herself. There was still time to change her mind. Still time to opt for his original punishment...

Mr Stanley read her thoughts. 'Very well, I shall contact your husband if that's what you wish me to do.'

'No, not that...'

'Then be so good as to do as you're told.'

'Couldn't I just stand here...?'

'You most certainly could not. Bend over, exactly as I said.'

Eventually, very red in the face and with a deep sigh of resignation, she began to bend forward from the waist, slowly and reluctantly, still stunned by the unreality of her situation, still hoping it might be a dream. Further and further she bent, the top of the chair digging into her stomach, her long blonde hair tumbling in front of her eyes, and the already well-filled seat of her short blue skirt tightening by degrees. At last she was sufficiently bent over so that she could place both hands, palms down, on the far side of the tabletop. While in that position she paused, hoping to give herself a little more time to adjust to the embarrassment and humiliation.

'Is there anything wrong?' he asked.

'I'm just composing myself,' she murmured over her shoulder.

'Well, I suggest you don't take too long.'

She took a deep breath. Her head was still a good eighteen inches above the table, yet she knew that her bottom was already raised in an extremely indelicate manner. This was undoubtedly the most undignified thing she'd ever had to do, she sighed to herself.

'I'm a patient man,' he continued, 'but I'd strongly advise you not to take unnecessary risks. Not in your present position, at least.'

Jennie decided there was little point in demurring any further. Sooner or later she'd have to bend right over the back of the chair in the manner he'd demanded. So it might as well be sooner. Closing her eyes she began to stretch forward and downward with the upper half of her body, hoping that the pressure from the top of the chair would ease once her head and elbows were firmly on the tabletop. She tried hard not to think of the spectacle she was being forced to make of herself, but she could sense his eyes all over the cheeks of her bottom as she continued to bend. She gasped. Ouch! The top of the chair was really cutting into the lower half of her midriff. But there wasn't too much further for her to go now. Her elbows were already safely on the table. It was just a matter of getting her head down there too - while Mr Stanley continued to stare at her lewdly displayed backside. It was as well she was wearing high heels, otherwise she'd never have been able to manage. It was also a good thing that she was quite an athletic girl who played badminton and squash three or four times a week, plus various other sports...

At last she was in the pose he required. At full stretch and on the very tips of her toes, but in the pose he required. Mr Stanley had judged the relative heights of the wooden chair, writing table, and school secretary to absolute perfection. The latter was now comprehensively draped over the former, her head down and the fullest, fleshiest part of her bottom almost at the pinnacle of her pose. A pose of which he'd dreamed for so long. The submissionary position, it might so well be called. With her feet and legs close together, the perfect half crescent of her buttocks was now thrust a good four inches higher than her head - exactly as he'd insisted.

Mr Stanley lounged back in his chair, fully satisfied with her stance and able to relax and relish the scene. And what a scene it was to be sure! Her short, dark-blue skirt had ridden right up to the swell of her buttocks, revealing the backs of two firm, perfectly rounded thighs that seemed to stretch down and down forever. The delightful contours of her bottom were now even more discernible than ever through the thin, tautly drawn material of her skirt. The very self-same bottom, he thought to himself, that had in the past tormented him so greatly. On occasions its plumpness and perfection had given him a real physical pain. But now he could gaze at it and experience only contentment and anticipation. Soon it would be held strictly to account for the intense frustration it had inflicted over the previous eighteen months. For the way it joggled and swayed under his gaze, taunting him and provoking him as it had gone - defiantly poking fun at his helpless condition, at his inability to deal with it in the way it so richly deserved. How had she dared to be so bold? How had she dared to parade such breathtaking beauty before his eyes, day after frustrating day, so brazenly, yet expect not to pay the price?

Jennie twisted her head to the left and glanced through a swathe of hair. She groaned in dismay. There, in the glass front of the bookcase, was the reflection of the lower half of her body. There she was, bent almost double over the back of the chair, her bottom raised and the hem of her smart blue skirt all the way up to the tops of her legs! Maybe even higher! What an unseemly picture she presented! She'd better look away at once - and keep on looking away, otherwise she'd simply die of embarrassment and shame!

She closed her eyes and took a deep breath. She supposed that any moment now he'd get up from his desk and start to lay that cruel cane across her far-too-lightly covered behind. She dreaded to think how much it was going to hurt...

But for the next ten minutes Mr Stanley sat at his desk, silent and still, his eyes riveted to the view. From the tousled top of her head, along the graceful sweep of her spine, up and over the twin peaks of her bottom, and then rapidly down to the toes of her high heel shoes, she was all he'd ever dreamed, and more. The epitome of total submission, offering herself up for sacrifice. Stretched to capacity and offering herself to him over the sacrificial altar of writing table and chair. He had to restrain the very strong impulse to leap to his feet there and then and bring the cane down across the exquisitely filled seat of her skirt with all his might. That would never do. He had to take his time if he was going to gain maximum satisfaction from this once-in-a-lifetime opportunity.

So he'd sit and study the backs of her legs once again. They were smooth and shapely, and bare because the summer day was far too hot for stockings and suspenders. Of course he'd always known she had long, lovely legs. But in her present stance their beauty was beyond belief. They were displayed to maximum advantage by the way she was obliged to stand on tiptoes in order to bend over the top of the chair and then right down to the table. And her skirt had risen so high that every splendid centimetre was visible. Suddenly it had been transformed from a mini to a micro-mini skirt. It was now no more than a pelmet around her buttocks. Indeed it was scarcely that. Another millimetre higher and he would have been afforded his first tantalising glimpse of honey-smooth cheeks and tiny, over-stretched knickers. And because she was at such stretch herself, every muscle in her legs, and above, was fully toned to its best.

Jennie kept her eyes closed. This was just so, so, so degrading. Fancy having to stand like this, letting him gawp at her upthrust hindquarters for as long as he wanted.

Was her skirt long enough to hide all the essentials? Or was the plumply filled crotch of her knickers peeping shyly out at him?

Oh, what a truly awful state of affairs!

'Now then, Mrs Jamieson, I want you to unzip your skirt, if you please. Unzip your skirt and then let it slide all the way down to the floor. But be sure to keep yourself bent right over the chair whilst doing so. Don't lift your head by so much as a fraction of an inch.'

Jennie felt the blood in her veins start to freeze. 'Mr Stanley,' she gasped in dismay, 'there's no need for that. No need at all.'

'Oh, but there certainly is, so kindly do just as you're told.'

'But I'm not wearing much underneath. Not very much at all.'

'Don't worry. I can assure you that I won't be offended.'

'But it really is next to nothing at all.'

'In that case I'm greatly looking forward to seeing for myself.'

'It can't really be necessary...?'

'I'm afraid that it can, and is.'

'This skirt's made of such lightweight material,' she persisted. 'It couldn't possibly make any difference.'

'It would make a great deal of difference, young lady. Kindly do just as I ask.'

'Mr Stanley, please, I shall die of embarrassment. Please show a little pity.'

'There's no shred of that in me, I'm very glad to say. As you'll find out soon enough. Even sooner, if you persist in arguing the point.'

'It really isn't thick enough to give me any protection at all.'

'Mrs Jamieson!' he barked. 'You're making me very cross!'

'Do I really have to do it?'

'I'll give you three guesses,' he hissed menacingly, standing up and swishing the cane through the air. 'But by the time you get to the second one you'll already know the answer.'

She heard him take a step in her direction. 'All right,' came the almost instant response. 'I'm unzipping it right now...'

'That's much better,' he said.

With her forehead still resting on the mahogany table she began to pluck, two-handed, at the right side of the waistband. 'I think the zip's stuck,' she puffed after a while.

'I warned you, Mrs Jamieson,' he growled, cutting the cane through the air once more.

'It's not my fault,' she wailed in alarm, tugging desperately at the zip fastener. 'It's nothing to do with me!'

'Is it not? I detest unequivocal statements based upon an inaccurate set of facts.' Again the cane hissed viciously just behind her upraised bottom.

Panic-stricken, she twisted her head and looked back at him. 'I'm doing my best. Really, I am. If only you'd let me stand up to do it I'd... oh, that's better. That's got it. Phew! It's completely undone now.'

'I'm so glad - for your sake,' he said coldly. 'Now, no more procrastination. Down it comes without any further delay.'

'It's a bit difficult in this position. Please be a little more patient.'

'Patience is not one of my myriad virtues.'

'Please wait a moment. It'll be easy once I've managed to wriggle the waistband over the top of the chair...'

'Yes, I can understand the problem there. But you seem to be coping quite well now. That's it. I think you've done it at last. Now, just let it slide all the way down to your feet... go on. Let go of it, Mrs Jamieson. Let go of it this instant.'

'M-Mr Stanley,' she stammered, 'it really is far too thin to offer me any kind of protection...'

'Let go of it now,' he insisted.

'You're absolutely sure?'

'One more word,' he threatened, whacking the cane down on the tabletop beside her and making her jump with fright. 'Just one more word, young lady.'

'I'm sorry. I didn't mean it. Look, I'm letting go of it now.'

As indeed she did. The skirt crumpled to the floor in sad, silent surrender, instantly revealing just how truthful she'd been concerning her lack of cover underneath. Mr Stanley's eyes bulged in delight and he had to swallow hard, several times, before he could trust to the normality of his voice. 'They are small, aren't they?' he breathed at last. 'Exceptionally small...'

Mr Stanley returned to his chair and sat rigidly to attention, staring across the eight feet or so of space that separated him from the tiny black triangle of semi-transparent knicker material that was stretched to capacity across the very centre of her perfect bottom. Across the very cheekiest part of the very cheekiest part of her perfect, pearly-pink bottom.

The sheer and utter sauciness of the spectacle before him simply defied belief. He decided there and then to administer a few extra cuts of the cane by way of sweet revenge. The sheer, brazen impertinence of that frothy little garment made him a very angry man indeed. For two pins he'd charge over there this instant and crack the cane down across the middle of it!

But he didn't. With an enormous effort of will he remained seated at his desk, cane still in hand, struggling to control his breathing.

Jennie, in the meantime, kept her eyes tightly shut with mortification. This was undoubtedly the most hideous day of her life. The most hideously embarrassing and degrading day of her life. If only the floor would open and swallow her up. Fancy having to bend right over this high-backed chair, with her bottom thrust way up high - and in Mr Stanley's direction! That in itself was bad enough, but when her poor bottom was covered by only the very flimsiest pair of see-through knickers... and 'covered' was hardly the right word. Most of her cheeks were well and truly outside the wretched little things. For all the good they did, they might just as well not exist at all. Whatever must she look like? Thank goodness the glass in the lower half of the window was opaque. At least no one else could see her plight. Why oh why didn't she ever wear a decent, respectable pair of panties? Mind you, it had never once crossed her mind that she'd ever find herself in this predicament. How could it have done? Not even when she'd been driving to work earlier that morning, knowing that something might well be said about last night's little misadventure. At worst she'd expected a few harsh words of rebuke. Never anything remotely like this...

It was just rotten luck that she'd chosen these particular knickers when she'd got dressed earlier. She had dozens of pairs of non-transparent ones at home. All of them really tiny, yes, but definitely *not* all of them see-through. If only she'd picked one of those from her knicker drawer. But she'd slipped slowly and sexily into these because she'd sensed Michael watching her from the bed behind. And she'd known they were his all-time favourites. So she used them to treat him to a sort of striptease in reverse. She'd already given him a really special blowjob that morning, in an effort to ease her conscience over the way she'd been so weak with Mr Parker the night before...

Oh dear! If only she could just keep thinking about her lovely Michael, it would help to take her mind away from the intense indignity of her current situation. And also from the terrifying thought of what Mr Stanley had promised to do to her. But she couldn't. Every so often her imagination kept straying back to the horrifying image of Mr Stanley angrily raising that long, hideous-looking cane above her poor, unprotected posterior.

Oh, how bad she felt about everything! About having been unfaithful to Michael, she meant. About him lying in bed that morning admiring her bare bottom as she'd slowly wriggled her way into these minuscule knickers. Admiring it in much the same way that Mr Parker had done when she'd been spread over that laboratory bench just a few short hours before. And in the same way, too, that Mr Stanley was undoubtedly doing right now, only a little over one hour later...

Yes, how bad she felt about what she'd done with Mr Parker. 'What an arse,' he'd gloated coarsely, standing behind her and utilising both hands to explore her bare cheeks, slowly and very methodically. 'What a beautiful, beautiful arse.' Which, at the time, had seemed and felt rather nice.

'Thank you,' she replied, blushing slightly.

'Turn your head and see what it's done to me,' he suggested, having temporarily removed his hands from the warmth of her bottom in order to step out of his tracksuit trousers.

'Gosh!' she'd murmured, genuinely impressed as well as eagerly anticipating events.

But what a change for her now. Just look at the grotesque situation in which she found herself now. How in heaven's name had all this come about? How on earth had she let it happen? How could she possibly be in such a predicament? How was it remotely possible that she should find herself bending right over this chair, all but bare of bottom, waiting to see whether or not the Headmaster intended to remove her knickers before he began to thrash her with that long, whippy cane? That long, whippy cane which she knew would slice deeply into her buttocks...

Well, possible or not, it most certainly had happened. In the first place she'd accepted - eventually - that he was deadly serious and that she had no alternative but to let him punish her in the way he wanted. Then, very slowly and reluctantly, she'd bent all the way over, exactly as he ordered, crimson-faced with shame. And then, even more reluctantly and with some considerable difficulty, she unzipped her smart blue skirt and dropped it all the way down to her feet, thereby unveiling almost every centimetre of her bottom to his hungry gaze. Had there ever been a point at which she might have saved herself? For the life of her, she couldn't think of one...

After what seemed an eternity of silence, she heard him stand up from his chair. But she didn't dare to risk another glance back. Cane in hand he approached the apparition of pink, creamy-smooth flesh and filmy black knickers, and took up a position behind and to the left of her raised cheeks. He'd chosen the spot carefully, in order to ensure that she remained fully in the light from the window.

'Well then,' he announced almost pleasantly, 'it's time to lay everything bare.'

Once again she closed her eyes and tried to wish herself out of the room. How embarrassing. How hideously, horribly embarrassing. She wasn't going to be allowed to retain even that tiny fragment of cover. That last remaining vestige of respectability. Was there to be no end to her torment? Oh, how she wished she could be somewhere else in the world. Anywhere else would do.

'Not that it looks likely to prove particularly heavy work,' he continued, closely inspecting the almost non-existent item of wearing apparel.

But still the wish wasn't granted. Still she remained in the room, bent uncomfortably over the chair. Still her far-too-prominently displayed rear was under close scrutiny. In fact, it was under even closer scrutiny than before. She was sure she could feel Mr Stanley's breath on the small of her back, just below the hem of her blouse.

So far as Mr Stanley was concerned, he was still in the same dilemma that had plagued him ever since her skirt had slipped prettily down her legs some ten minutes beforehand. There was only one way to resolve it, he decided. Mentally he would have to toss a coin. Heads, he'd order her to remove the knickers herself, just as she had the skirt. Tails, and he'd do the job for her.

It came down tails in his mind.

Very well. So be it. He'd uncover her himself. She'd have found either method equally demeaning, so it didn't really matter that much. And as he was to be in charge of removing that final scrap of respectability, he could at least make it last as long as he wanted. To start with he'd tease her a little...

'You must admit I've been very patient,' he said, using the tip of the cane to ping her knicker elastic.

'Oh!' she squealed in surprise and alarm, risking a quick look over her shoulder and spotting the cane in his hand.

'But time is rapidly running out. You'll appreciate there is much that has still to be done?'

'Oh, er, um...'

'And I'm sure your good husband, were he here, would wish to see it done properly. After all, it is for his benefit. He's the one who's been deceived by these parts.' By way of emphasis he ran the tip of the cane, very lightly, across the scarcely knickered cheeks of her gorgeous bottom. 'It was his slice of them that you gave away so gleefully last night in the chemistry laboratory. His, and nobody else's. And he can't get it back now, can he, poor fellow? It's gone from him once and for all.'

Jennie was tempted to retort, but sensibly decided to hold her tongue.

'I don't hear any objections,' he said after a silence of half a minute. 'To the laying bare of these parts, I mean. I thought you might protest.'

'Would it do any good if I did?'

'None whatsoever. Much the opposite, in fact. It would simply add to the misery to come.'

He adjusted his stance and again reached out with the cane. 'This little snippet of knicker nonsense has angered me for long enough. It's high time it was dispatched once and for all. Not that I would expect you to agree, of course.'

So saying, he poked the tip of the cane into the top of the ample cleft that separated each smoothly rounded cheek. Then slowly but surely he ran it downwards, making her shudder, until the oh-so-petite panties were drawn, inexorably, away from her sweetly blushing bottom. He paused for a moment, stepping back to admire the way he'd left them clinging decoratively to the very tops of her thighs.

'A rather ticklish matter,' he joked, emphasising his meaning by running the tip of the cane back up the valley between her buttocks, 'but a satisfactory conclusion. And that's the bottom line... and so, of course, is this. And a very pretty one it is, too. It seems to go on forever. I love the way it runs from here all the way up to here... and then, of course, all the way back down to here again.'

'Oh, um... *Mr* Stanley—'

'And those cheeks. So delightfully dimpled. So full and rounded. So plump, yet firm and pert. The whole creation really is perfection personified.'

Jennie closed her eyes and groaned inwardly with humiliation. The horrible little man was standing there behind her, talking animatedly about her totally bare bottom...

'The trouble with such perfection,' he continued, with noticeably less warmth than before, 'is that it tends to annoy and then infuriate. It tends to harden the heart and lend considerable weight to the arm that wields the cane. As you will shortly discover.'

Without further ado he reached forward with the cane and guided the already displaced panties all the way down to her ankles. 'No more chit-chat, Mrs Jamieson,' he snapped, tapping the cane purposefully across the middle of her pouting cheeks and making them joggle in a most intriguing manner. 'Now I must concentrate on finding the very best method of roasting this fat little arse alive!'

Part Two

As Mr Stanley began to run the cane slowly and very deliberately back and forth over bare, silky-smooth cheeks - pausing momentarily when it lay across the timidly quivering high points in order to emphasise to himself exactly where he intended to place the first searing stroke - Jennie again tried to close her mind to her desperate situation and pretend she was somewhere else. Any place at all. Any place in the world where her naked nether regions would not be so shamefully on show. Any place where they would not be under such fearsome threat. But it simply wasn't possible. She couldn't even divert her mind for more than a couple of seconds. Her present plight was all too real. Particularly because of the way Mr Stanley was continuing to caress her with the cane.

She stared down at the highly polished mahogany tabletop that was almost touching the tip of her nose, and sighed heavily to herself. She took back all she'd said. Every single word. About the knickers, she meant. About saying they were no good at all. Tiny and transparent though they might be, they were still much, much, much better than no knickers at all. She'd give anything in the world to have them back in place right now. There was just no way of describing how exposed and vulnerable she felt. She'd willingly pay him a thousand pounds out of her own bank account to have that teeny-weeny morsel of comfort back where it belonged.

It wasn't that she'd never been knickerless in the presence of someone other than her husband. It hadn't happened very often, of course, but she had to admit that in six years of marriage it had occurred more than once prior to last night. Try as one might, it just wasn't possible to avoid that sort of thing entirely. Not when one's rear end was constantly being hunted by a whole variety of ruthless men. But those previous panty-free experiences had been totally different, of course. For a start, the other man hadn't been intending to lacerate her bottom with a long, wicked cane...

Although, to be truthful, there had been those ninety minutes she'd spent at Westminster police station two years ago, after the massage parlour debacle. And also the time when that cheeky Jonathan Crowe put her over his knee - right in front of her husband's other business partner, Chris Poole. But that had only been a bit of gentle fun... well, fairly gentle, anyway...

Okay. All right. It had been hard and painful if the whole sordid truth had to be told. But the aftermath was certainly fun. She'd never felt so turned on and ready for a spot of naughty. Unfortunately both men were more than willing and able to provide...

Oh dear! If only she could expect that this time she'd be able to escape with nothing worse than an overheated bottom and her virtue slightly dented. But that was out of the question. She was quite sure that Mr Stanley meant every word of every threat. Every word, and more beside.

Help! Mr Stanley had just lowered the cane and started running it slowly over the backs of her thighs! She hoped this new move wasn't significant. Surely he had no evil intent towards that part of her person as well?

After a while Mr Stanley returned his attention to the ripeness of her buttocks. He'd make up his mind about her legs in a while. In the meantime he'd concentrate on the primary target. A firm, fleshy target, the sheer wanton beauty of which was making him angrier and angrier by the minute. Such impudent perfection could only be dealt with in one way.

Mind you, by the time he'd finally dealt with it his anger and frustration would be a thing of the past, buried once and for all. In the months and years that lay ahead he'd be able to gaze at that impertinent bottom and feel nothing but a warm, deep glow of intense satisfaction.

But that was in the future. Right now there was a job to be done. A very important job. One that had to be executed to the best of his ability, because the opportunity would never occur again. So he'd allow his anger to escalate while he took stock and savoured the sweetness of the moment.

And not only must he savour it. He must store it away in his memory so that he'd be able to recall every graphic detail at will. What a picture she made, bent over by the window. Bent over and awaiting the cane. A picture of two stark contrasts, in fact. From the nape of her neck to the small of her back she was respectably clothed in a white satin blouse that ended, tightly and elegantly, around the slimmest part of her waist. But from there down to her high heels not a stitch adorned her. Not a single, solitary stitch. Bare buttocks reared right in front of him... almost literally under his nose. Bare, immaculately shaped buttocks that trembled nervously in their unaccustomed exposure to the full light of the working day. Bare, immaculately shaped buttocks that were now, at his insistence, the highest part of her above the carpet...

And what a magnificent part they were too! So outrageously proud and insolent in their nakedness. So painful in their perfection... and so slippery-smooth and flawless, that in the glare of light from the window they shimmered and shone like highly polished porcelain...

This was not the bottom of some naughty teenage schoolgirl. These were mature-woman buttocks, delightfully full and fleshy, sculpted to perfection, and dimpled so impishly in the centre of each glossy cheek. Buttocks that, over the years, had been carefully tended with expensive creams and oils. Buttocks so pampered and petted that their texture was buttery smooth. Buttocks so unsullied and free from blemish that they positively screamed out for the cane. And buttocks that must have afforded her husband almost unendurable pleasure ever since the first time he'd unwrapped them and taken possession.

And at least one other person had sampled them since then. He knew for certain that Mr Parker had recently taken his fill. And to his mind it seemed unlikely that Mr Parker was the only one ever to trespass upon them. There must have been one or two others before? One or two others who'd also managed to poach them. One or two others who'd also been allowed to pillage and plunder these bare, bouncy buttocks that gleamed so appealingly as she bent over the back of the chair, head low and bottom high, fearfully awaiting her fate.

How had it been last night for Mr Parker? How had it been when he had her, bottoms up, across that laboratory bench? How had he thrilled to the way he was ramming his stomach and groin into those bountiful buttocks, whilst impaling and stretching her insides?

Had anyone ever shagged that beautiful bottom? It was such an inviting shape that he wouldn't be at all surprised to learn that someone had insisted on fucking her there...

Jennie groaned to herself once again. The interminable waiting was almost unbearable. Why didn't he do or say something? This was as much of an ordeal as the actual caning would be. Well... almost as much - in a different sort of a way. She rather wished he'd get started. It had to happen sometime, so it might as well happen now. At least once it was over she'd be allowed into an upright stance and then back into her clothes.

Whatever was he doing? It must have been a good ten minutes since he'd stopped stroking the cane all over her bottom and upper thighs. He was just standing there, silent and still. She could feel his eyes all over her bottom - a physical presence, almost as if they'd been his hands. What could he be thinking about? Oh dear, how hideously embarrassing if he were standing there staring at the cheeks of her bare bottom and trying to visualise exactly how they'd been mounted so massively in the chemistry lab last night. She'd simply die of shame! Oh gosh, what a really terrible thought! She'd better try to convince herself that Mr Stanley wasn't that sort of person. Although, to be honest, she strongly suspected he was.

Deep in thought Mr Stanley held the cane, once again, across the middle of her upthrust bottom, making her quiver with fright. No, he said to himself, this wasn't some naughty sixteen-year-old schoolgirl whose bare buttocks were on display - a heart-stopping display that started immediately below the hem of her blouse. No, this was a respectable married woman of twenty-eight, with four-year-old twin sons at private school and a well-heeled husband who was a professional man in town. An architect, in fact, and also a highly respected member of local society. Round Table, Rotary, Lions club, and all that sort of thing. And, come to think of it, one of the Conservative candidates for the local elections next month.

Now here was a very fine thought. What would his electorate think if they could see his dear wife right now? The wife of their prospective Tory councillor, bare-arsed and waiting to be beaten! Humbled and waiting to be hurt! How would that affect his election chances?

And what of his own views, were the gentleman in question standing directly behind his dear wife? What would he think if he could see her headmaster measuring her up for the ordeal ahead? How would he react if he could perceive her present plight? If he could study the quaking of these spectacular buttocks beside which he awoke every morning? Would he lend his wholehearted support to the punishment ahead, if he knew the full reasons for it? Would he wish to add a few extra strokes of his own? He rather suspected the answer to both those last two questions was very much in the affirmative. Yes, it would be fascinating to have the gentleman here and to be able to see right into his mind...

And what of her lady friends, too? That was another fascination - those co-members of Ladies Circle, Inner Wheel and similar organisations. Those expensively groomed young mothers who basked in the prosperity they'd wed. Those elegant young wives who attended umpteen coffee mornings, jumble sales and PTA meetings, chattering ceaselessly about their possessions and their pricey new acquisitions, and how they would never dream of going to Spain on holiday because it was so terribly over-commercialised. What would they say if they could see this one of their number at this precise moment in time? Wouldn't it be wonderful if they could all be present to witness her total humiliation? This highly respected member of their ranks who'd been so painstakingly stripped and prepared for the cane. Imagine the outrage! Particularly from the feminists amongst them. How gratifying it would be to have them all lined up behind him. Not only at the current moment, but also when the cane was weaving its evil spell. 'Would anyone else care for a taste?' he could enquire politely after raising yet another red welt. 'If so there's a perfectly good desk over there, and I can be with you as soon as you like.' Mind you, no one would be able to hear him above the din his school secretary would be making.

Jennie was suddenly struck with a thought even more horrifying than Mr Stanley standing there picturing just how Mr Parker had made such a meal of her last night; a thought that simply hadn't occurred to her before. She knew that what she was about to receive would be no ordinary spanking. No common or garden slapping of her bottom, the worst effects of which were gone in twenty-four hours or so. No, that thin, venomous-looking cane was going to inflict untold agonies on the soft, bouncy cheeks of her bottom...

Of course she'd understood that much all along - ever since the awful shock of realising his intentions toward her. That wasn't what suddenly disturbed her so greatly. No, her current alarm was due to the realisation that the cane would leave its mark across her bottom for days rather than hours, and there was no way in the world that she was going to be able to hide that from Michael. After all, much of his time at home was spent with one or both hands inside the seat of her knickers. Not that she objected, of course. It was lovely to have a really passionate hunk of a husband who was constantly upending her in every corner of the house... and garden. But it did mean she was in trouble. Far, far greater trouble than she'd appreciated only a few moments ago.

What earthly reason could she give Michael for coming home with her bottom lined with stripes? Raised, ugly red stripes that wouldn't be able to bear even the lightest of touches. He'd know immediately that something was wrong when she was obliged to dodge out of the way of his customary 'good evening' slap and tickle. What could she do? Once he discovered she'd been extensively caned he would, quite naturally, go ballistic.

Perhaps she could pretend she was suffering from some sort of peculiar allergy? Well, that was a bit thin, she supposed. Whoever had heard of such a thing? But it might be better than no excuse at all. Could she persuade that rather fanciable Dr Osborne to back up her story? No, she guessed she couldn't. He had professional ethics to concern himself with, after all. Although, if she were to be really sweet and sexy with him...

No, that was no good. Michael wasn't daft. Far from it. Even with the help of some tame quack he'd never accept it. There was no way he'd ever mistake the telltale effects of the cane.

So she'd simply have to conceal it from him. There was no other way out from under. But how could she conceivably do that?

Unless she left him for a week...

That was a bit drastic, but it might be better than facing the music. She could always say she'd had some sort of mental breakdown.

No, he wouldn't believe that either. He'd suspect she'd been with another man, and that would be just as bad, or worse. And anyway, there were the children to think about.

Now here was a possibility! Suppose, just suppose, she took to her bed with 'flu'? Suppose she stayed there until all the marks had gone, pretending she was too ill to move? Surely that was a possibility? Surely it could be made to work? Michael could take the boys to school, and her mother would collect them as usual. And if Mr Stanley didn't like her taking sick leave, then tough! He could always do what they do in Hastings - go and stick his head up a dead bear's bum!

Yes, it was a definite possibility. Indeed, it was the only possibility that sprung to mind. It wouldn't be easy, of course, but with a little ingenuity it just might succeed in saving her hide... or what little was going to be left of it to save...

Mr Stanley took a deep breath. His plans had been laid meticulously, and he was almost ready to begin. He could visualise exactly how it would be when he did. The first and unkindest cut of all would be laid right across the fattest part of her bottom - across the high point of each polished cheek. Three separate sounds would merge into one as he struck: the hiss of the cane through the air, the short, sharp, fleshy crack as it landed slap-bang on target, and the instantaneous yelp of pain. As if by magic a magnificent red welt would suddenly be raised, exactly along the line where the cane had bitten so deeply a split second earlier.

After that first scalding stroke he'd wait until the sobbing had subsided and she was weeping in semi-silence. Then he'd strike again, just above or below the first cut. This process would be patiently repeated until those pale, pouting cheeks that gleamed up at him so invitingly were colourfully decorated with twelve thick, agonisingly painful welts. Twelve thick, agonisingly painful welts as parallel to and equi-distant from each other as the accuracy of his aim would allow. Then, after a suitable pause to admire his handiwork, and to lure her into a false sense of security, he'd paint her with a few more - in retaliation for the audacity she'd shown in exposing herself to him in just that tiny triangle of see-through knicker material. He'd paint her with a few more across the very tops of her thighs, laid with the same severity as he'd earlier applied to these infuriatingly honey-smooth cheeks. Cheeks so steeped in recent adultery that its stigma was almost a physical thing.

But enough of that for the moment. The time for action had arrived at last. The time for wreaking revenge on those saucily displayed cheeks that positively dripped with last night's infidelity.

'These parts have sinned!' he exclaimed angrily, pressing the length of the cane firmly across the fullest part of her buttocks, and noting with approval the pretty indentation it made along the line of the intended cut. 'Not only have they sinned against the trust and authority that others have placed in me, but they have also sinned against your lawful wedded husband. They have failed disgracefully in their duty to keep themselves only unto him. But fear not, I shall grant them absolution. I shall purify them with fire!' He raised the cane on high, carefully taking aim. 'I shall purify them with a fire so intense they'll think twice before ever sinning again!'

So saying, he brought the cane down in a hissing arc that homed in with deadly accuracy towards the duly appointed target of those soft, shiny, and oh-so-vulnerable twin peaks.

Part Three

Just as Mr Stanley predicted, the intensely satisfying crack of cane across fleshy bare buttocks was almost instantly drowned by the equally satisfying yelp of agonised outrage. Tears sprang from her eyes as she sobbed with her mouth open wide.

'Be silent, Mrs Jamieson,' he warned. 'Do you want the whole school to know that your bare bottom is being caned for the way it was found fornicating on school premises last night?'

Jennie clenched her teeth and clamped both hands over her mouth, but was unable to stifle the sound of her distress completely. 'That's better,' said the headmaster. 'In future you will make every effort to contain yourself after each stroke of the cane. Otherwise I shall prolong your ordeal until you learn how to obey me.'

Mr Stanley stared with delight at the monstrously thick red welt that had suddenly appeared right across the widest part of her otherwise flawless bottom. And the more he stared the more his excitement grew. This was the only way to deal with an ill-disciplined young lady, he gloated to himself. This was the only way. You made her bend over the back of a chair and obliged her to suffer the gradual and highly undignified baring of her upturned bottom. Then, after making her wait for what must have seemed an eternity, you sliced the cane right across the middle with all your might. No compromise was permitted. No element of clemency allowed. You sliced the long, heavy cane down across the ripeness of her upthrust buttocks with every single ounce of strength you possessed. And then you kept on slicing it...

Mr Stanley balanced the cane comfortably in his right hand and waited patiently for the sobbing to subside. Only then, when he gauged the moment to be absolutely right, would he strike again and raise a second red-hot line across her.

Mr Stanley gazed intently at the bare bottom that now carried the blazing red insignia of his cane across its very centre. The bare bottom that writhed urgently from side to side, as if to cool itself. It would take a long while to complete the caning, he thought. Almost half an hour, he imagined. But it would be much, much longer before this unbelievably cheeky young lady would be able to bear even the flimsiest pair of knickers against her sorely wounded rear. It might well be days before she'd be able to tolerate that. And the twelve straight lines he intended to paint would be with her for as long as a week.

'Oh, *God*,' gasped Jennie, tears running down her face. 'Oh God that hurts!

That really, really hurts! You can't believe how much...'

He held the back of his hand against the ridged welt, checking the heat for himself. 'Do you consider it to be any more than you deserve, Mrs Jamieson?'

'I don't know...'

'Would you care for a little more time to get over your distress?'

'Oh, yes please,' she gasped with relief.

Stealthily he raised the cane on high. 'Well that's not a problem,' he murmured. 'That's not a problem at all. Take just as much time as you like.'

'Thank you, Mr Stanley.'

He smiled sadistically to himself as he measured his aim with great care. The very unexpectedness of this next stroke should significantly enhance the effect.

Jennie howled up at the ceiling, her feet jumping several inches off the floor as the cane bit savagely across both cheeks, causing them to bounce up and down.

'Silence,' he commanded. 'Can you not remember what I said?'

Mr Stanley gazed down at the two red and white welts now painted so prettily across the very fleshiest part of her buttocks. The two wicked red and white welts - both over a quarter of an inch in height - that absolutely burst with colour and life, that positively radiated rude good health. Each one was covered with a mass of white goose bumps, a tribute to the searing heat of the welt compared to the relative chill of the room.

Yes, that was much better, he thought. Much, much better indeed. More than twice as good as before. He was mightily confident that those licentious little mounds of flesh were now significantly less keen on a spot of adultery. Significantly less keen to be mounted than they had been twelve or so hours before, when they'd been bent over in the chemistry lab and offered up to Mr Parker in very much the same pose as at present. But what a contrast for this ill-disciplined young lady! What a difference for her between last night's pose and today's! Last night's pose of lustful desire, and today's of pain and humiliation.

Mr Stanley glared down balefully at the ripe cheeks that offended him so greatly. It was incredibly rewarding to see how well he'd marked them already, with a mere two cuts of the cane. Now they were far from their former selves. Their perfection was already a thing of the past. Now, as they trembled and pulsed in fear and pain, each cheek bore the most magnificent hallmark of his authority right across its fullest part. And the hallmark was going to grow. It was going to grow massively. Ten more lines were going to be added. Ten more burning, blistering lines...

Then he'd deal with the tops of her legs. One stroke immediately after the other, in stark contrast to the way he was taking his time to punish her beautiful bottom.

When he finally completed the caning he'd leave her whilst he finished some paperwork. He'd leave her bent over the back of the chair, bare bottomed and tearful, while he worked at his desk, casting the not-so-occasional glance in her direction. He'd leave her there until the tears and the snuffling stopped completely. He'd leave her in that highly undignified pose until she'd recovered her composure as far as she could. Then, after another five minutes or so he'd say, very smoothly, 'Mrs Jamieson, would you mind covering yourself up and collecting your notebook and pencil. There are a few messages I'd like you to deliver to the staff. Then you're to report to Miss Stricton in her office. I know she'll be anxious to see for herself exactly how justice has been done. She may even wish to add a little more justice of her own.'

Mr Stanley cocked his head to one side and stared with careful consideration at the pouting twin globes that had - until a short while before - been so impeccably unsullied. Whence should he direct the next excruciating contact between school secretary and cane? Should it be along the line of the sweet little crease that divided buttocks from thighs? The cut that would cause her maximum discomfort whenever she moved. Or should it be just above the first scalding line? The first scalding line that was violently pulsating with pain, in common with the one he'd raised an inch below it. He'd take a little more time to decide...

Jennie was unable to slow the stream of tears, nor calm the wriggling of her hips. Oh God, she'd been mortally wounded. She'd never known pain like it. She'd never even imagined there could be pain like it. The cane seemed to cut her to the bone. It seemed to burn its way down into her flesh as far as it could possibly go.

As the fire continued to rage right across her she squeezed the tops of her legs together and gasped. Yes, just as she'd suspected, she was incredibly wet at the junction of her thighs. Wetter, by far, than she'd ever known. She could feel her internal juices trickling down the inside of each leg...

And now that she'd squeezed again she was starting to come! Very sharply, in fact. Very, very sharply. Suddenly her whole body was consumed by orgasm. Her insides were positively seething with pleasure!

Thank heavens she was still blubbering like a baby! Otherwise Mr Stanley might well have been able to tell what was happening to her. And how embarrassing that would be!

Good grief, she really was climaxing like mad! And of course she knew the reason why. The intensity of the pain inflicted had set her off more effectively than the world's finest fuck. How truly amazing. Her poor bottom was absolutely ablaze, yet the heat in her loins was almost as great. The external agony was being almost exactly counterbalanced by the internal delight. And much as she feared the next cruel laceration across her buttocks, she was fully aware that it might well make her spasm more fiercely than ever.

This was unreal! She was still crying an ocean of tears, yet she was simply wracked with orgasm. The sharpest, most delicious multi-orgasm she'd ever known. And now, in a really peculiar way, she was almost looking forward to the third cut from the cane, even though she was dreading further pain.

Oh, mother, she could sense that, behind her back, Mr Stanley was taking aim once again. She must clench her teeth and keep both hands over her mouth. Would the next streak of red-hot pain across both cheeks increase the strength of her climax even more? Or would it drive it away completely? She supposed she'd soon find out...

Part Four

Mr Stanley smiled thinly at the high-pitched screech of suffering as the cane rose and fell across those soft, round cheeks. Cheeks so shiny-smooth and immaculate just a short while before. Cheeks so totally free from flaw until they'd tasted the length of the cane across them. Now they were burnt and bouncing under his gaze - for the third time that morning. He gripped the cane tightly in his hand and drank deep of the wondrous sight and sound. Perhaps this would teach her a lesson. Perhaps this would teach her that if you were a young lady who possessed the most beautiful pair of buttocks imaginable, then you were well advised to hide them safely away under loose fitting wraps, and not flaunt them before the rest of the world in skirts that were too short and which fitted far too snugly across them? Personally, he rather suspected that by the time the cane finally finished punishing this exquisite bottom, the lesson would indeed be well and truly learnt.

Mr Stanley was delighted with his achievements thus far. The cane had sliced down into her so deeply, raising three ugly red welts right across the fullest part of each cheek. The second was raised approximately an inch below the first, whilst the third was a similar distance above it. All three vicious red lines were as parallel to each other as he could have hoped, showing considerable skill on his part, he told himself proudly. He could easily understand why she had problems stifling her sobs of dismay. Each throbbing welt was so suffused that anyone would be able to see the agony it was causing. A tribute not only to the weight of his arm, but also to the quality of the cane. He longed to raise a fourth, but it was too soon, he told himself firmly. He must be patient and wait for her to calm down further. That was the way in which to exact maximum retribution. Twelve strokes of the cane with an interval of two or three minutes between were many times more effective than twelve strokes one after the other. So he must hold back until the whimpering had virtually ceased. Then and only then would the cane be allowed to kiss her again.

Another wicked hiss. Another fleshy crack. Yet more howls of anguish as the cane cut venomously into and across the ripeness of her bottom. And yet another villainous red and white line to match the other three.

The pleasure she'd felt earlier had gone, leaving her with nothing but physical torment. Why was he doing this to her, she gasped to herself, her hands over her mouth and her face contorted with pain? Why was he hurting her so? What sort of enjoyment could he possibly gain through treating her so fiendishly? She was only too well aware that almost all men would welcome the opportunity to spank a shapely female bottom, but did they also harbour a secret desire to inflict this sort of brutality on it as well?

Mr Stanley stared joyfully down at her upthrust cheeks, at the four cruel marks that bore such testimony to the barbarity of the punishment. Never would he be able to gain a greater sense of euphoria. Never would he be able to find anything so gratifying as punishing those twin ovals so severely. Punishing them for the way they'd spent the last eighteen months wiggling and jiggling in front of him. For the way he'd had to watch the shameless, lightly clad cheeks sway their way around his school, teasing and tantalising him as they went. How had she ever imagined she'd be able to do that - day after long, frustrating day - yet not have to pay the price?

Well, now the price was most certainly being paid in full. Now these juicy-ripe cheeks that had incensed him so greatly were being held well and truly to account. Never would they be able to mock him again.

And it wasn't just the infliction of pain that was so rewarding. It was the intense humiliation, too. The humiliation he'd been able to heap upon her so prodigiously. Imagine how she must have felt; first having to bend low over the back of the chair, then having to suffer her beautiful bottom being bared by degrees, and finally having to wait for what must have seemed ages while he stood behind her, cane in hand, staring greedily at the naked, moon-shaped buttocks upon which he'd been so fully intent on exacting maximum revenge. The waiting and the consequent humiliation must have been as unbearable as the fire now raging across her. Well, almost as unbearable, anyway. This respectably married young mother of twins must have suffered untold agonies of mind whilst bared and bent forward in that way. She'd have known for sure and certain just how avidly his eyes were devouring her lewdly exposed bottom. She'd also have known for certain just how he'd been intending to deal with it. She'd have known, too, just how great a thrill he was experiencing at the sight of those gorgeous bare buttocks so hapless and helpless as they pouted right in front of him.

Oh yes, the price was being well and truly paid. The ghost was being well and truly laid. Accounts were being settled, debts repaid.

'I'm sorry,' she sniffed tearfully. 'I'm sorry about Mr Parker last night. It'll never happen again.'

'I'm extremely glad to hear it, Mrs Jamieson.'

'Please can you stop now? I don't think I can take any more.'

For the fifth time he raised the cane above his head. 'You're sorry, are you, young lady?'

'Oh yes, very, very sorry indeed.'

'Really? Very, very sorry, you say?'

'Yes, Mr Stanley, very, very sorry. Please, I just can't stand any more.'

'You just can't stand any more?'

'No, I can't stand any more pain. Please, Mr Stanley...'

He balanced the cane on the palm of his hand, carefully measuring his next strike. 'Well, I suppose I could show some leniency,' he said thoughtfully. 'I suppose it's not totally out of the question. I'm a compassionate and reasonable man, after all.'

'Oh, thank God for that.'

'But then, on the other hand...'

'Pardon, Mr Stanley?'

Crack! The cane bit her again, making her howl into her hands and writhe exactly as before - and making her headmaster even more erect than ever. Not that he had any inclination at all to fuck her. This was far more gratifying than the mere act of copulation. This was 'possessing' her in the true sense of the word.

'Six!' exclaimed Mr Stanley, pleased with the way his aim had been slightly off course, thereby causing the cane to cross over the last part of the welt immediately above and the first part of the one immediately below, and produce a greatly enhanced swelling where the two welts joined together. He cocked his head thoughtfully to one side... Yes. Yes, why not? He'd allow the same thing to happen with each of the final six strokes. The result was extremely rewarding. And the cruelty of the welt-on-welt effect had not been lost on the wayward young wife, judging by the prolonged shrieking and wriggling of hips.

'Halfway House, Mrs Jamieson,' he stated cheerfully. 'Time to return to my desk for a cigarette, before completing this onerous task. You stay just as you are, of course.'

She closed her eyes and blushed with embarrassment. 'Yes, Mr Stanley,' she gulped.

He sat upright in his chair, cigarette in one hand and the cane resting on the desktop in front of him. What a vision lay a few feet away to his right. That magnificent bare bottom bent over the back of the chair and burning brightly from the six times it had been caressed so sadistically by the cane. That magnificent bottom, ravished last night by Mr Parker, and now ravaged by the cane. It really was the most beautiful, most perfect, most caneable bottom imaginable...

What would be in her mind right now? Was she simply consumed with pain, or would her thoughts be on what was to come? Or was she wondering how she was going to conceal her predicament from her good husband?

Mr Stanley's gaze settled on his in-tray. 'What have you done with the sixth form geography rosters, Mrs Jamieson?' he enquired, as if nothing was out of the ordinary, yet addressing his question to the six red-hot lines that decorated her bottom so colourfully. 'I feel certain they were here on my desk yesterday afternoon.'

Once again she blushed with embarrassment, although not quite understanding why. 'I put them in the filing cabinet last night,' she mumbled.

'Under what?'

'Under G-R, for geography rosters.'

'You can get them for me later. Currently there are other concerns that require your attention.'

'Yes, Mr Stanley,' she whispered.

'Did you check the e-mails when you arrived at work?'

'Yes, Mr Stanley.'

'I don't suppose we have yet received the promised communication from Colonel Rice-Barton?'

'No, Mr Stanley.'

'Nor from General Fitzbourne-Williams?'

'No, Mr Stanley.'

'Perhaps you could check your in-box again when next you return to your room?'

'Yes, Mr Stanley.'

'They did promise to respond today, did they not?'

'Yes, Mr Stanley.'

'By what time?' he asked, still looking her full in the buttocks as he spoke.

She sensed the continued direction of his gaze and blushed even more deeply. Having him sitting behind her, talking quite normally about work - while she remained bent over the table - was somehow even worse than having him standing beside her, cane held menacingly in hand. And she suspected he was probably aware of that fact. 'B-by four o'clock, Mr Stanley,' she stammered.

'Remind me to phone them if we've heard nothing by then.'

'Yes, Mr Stanley.'

'In fact, I'll put it in my electronic diary as well.'

'That's a good idea, Mr Stanley.'

'How do I do that?'

'You click on *tasks*, Mr Stanley.'

'And then?'

'And then on today's date.'

'And then?'

'Then you just type yourself a reminder.'

'Thank you. I'll attend to that as soon as this current matter is concluded.'

'Yes, Mr Stanley.'

'Don't let me forget.'

'I won't, Mr Stanley.'

'And next time there are rosters on my desk, kindly do not file them until I place them in the filing basket.'

'No, Mr Stanley. I'm sorry.'

Five minutes of silence followed. Then he ground out his second cigarette and advanced on the spectacle of his miserably unhappy school secretary, staring down with renewed approval at the excellence of his handiwork to date. 'Now then, Mrs Jamieson,' he said sternly, laying the cane across the unsullied area of flesh he intended to incinerate next, and making her twitch with fright. 'I trust you have made use of the respite in order to reflect on the error of your ways?'

'Yes, Mr Stanley.'

'As well as the justness of this punishment?'

'Yes, Mr Stanley.'

'Lust is one of the seven deadly sins, is it not?'

'Yes, Mr Stanley.'

'And so is pride.'

'Yes, Mr Stanley.'

He raised the cane high above his head, aiming to angle the stroke across two of the others. 'You take great pride in the shape of these salacious cheeks, do you not?'

Jennie sensed the inherent danger. 'Oh, um, well...'

'Yes or no?' he pressed.

'Yes, Mr Stanley,' she hastened to reply.

'You're proud to parade them back and forth in tight skirts and trousers?'

'Yes, Mr Stanley,' she sighed with resignation.

'I rest my case,' he proclaimed, sweeping the cane down with all the power at his disposal...

'And, even more significantly, adultery is a breach of one of the Ten Commandments.'

'Yes, Mr Stanley.'

'Eight!'

Jennie screamed through hands and tightly clenched teeth yet again. Oh, God! The last three strokes had been even more painful than ever! They must have crossed over one or some of the others!

And yet she was so wet between her thighs. She must continue to keep them pressed tightly together. She didn't want Mr Stanley to see the reaction of her woefully wanton pussy.

'And so is coveting thy neighbour's wife.'

'That was Mr Parker...'

'The modern equivalent would be coveting thy neighbour's partner.'

'I suppose that could have been me...'

Crack! 'Nine!'

Mr Stanley was intrigued by the way each of the last four cuts had crisscrossed the beginning of one and the end of another. Now then, why not compound that welt-on-welt effect across the very widest part of her bottom? Why not aim the next three cuts to maximum advantage? Why not lay each of them, as far as possible, along the line of the first? Why not lay the last three, one after the other, slap-bang on top of the first? How exhilarating the result would be! And how desperately intense the suffering...

Some eight minutes later the twelfth and final stroke had been laid across her. Laid across her with the same savagery and accuracy as all those that had gone before. He'd performed his labour of love exactly as he'd intended. The plumpest part of each rounded cheek was now decorated with a multitude of bright red lines. A multitude of mammoth ridged welts, each covered with an array of white goose bumps as they throbbed and pulsed with heat and pain. A multitude of blazing welts, the lowest of which ran exactly along the crease that divided buttocks from thighs. From there the lateral marks of the cane ran upward and over the peak of each cheek.

The first five strokes he'd delivered lay parallel to each other and approximately the same distance apart. Each of the next four encroached upon two of the others at an angle, almost doubling the size of the swelling where they met.

But, oh, the final three! Those strokes had been so well directed that - across the very centre of her bottom - four welts overran each other! Four welts, one on top of the other at a very slight angle, across the highest point of her bottom, thus raising a monstrous contusion, the shape, size and colour of which was pure joy for Mr Stanley to behold.

The temptation was just too great for him. He laid the cane lightly across the area of engorged flesh and then lifted it carefully on high. 'You've heard of a baker's dozen, Mrs Jamieson?'

'Yes, Mr Stanley.'

'So you know what to expect now?'

'Yes, Mr Stanley.'

The cane whistled through the air and landed with an evil splat across the middle of the swelling, the resultant display of misery far from disappointing.

For several minutes he gazed down in awe at the glorious array of scarlet welts painted vividly and viciously right across the fleshiest area of each grief-stricken cheek. It was a sight that would remain with him for the rest of his life - the beautiful bottom that had previously tortured and tormented his soul now naked and writhing before him. Stripped bare and excruciatingly caned. Never would those saucily shaped buttocks be able to tease or tantalise him again. He'd always be able to watch them snaking their way around the school and recall their present plight. He'd always be able to recall the way in which he'd bent them right over the back of the chair and then bared them. Bared them slowly and with maximum shame and mortification. And he'd be able to recall how he'd then seared them thirteen times with his cane. Seared them so thoroughly that when he held the palms of his hands just above her he could actually feel the heat she was radiating. Oh, yes, the spectacle of this lovely caned bottom would be etched indelibly in his memory forever and a day...

Mr Stanley stood almost directly behind her, cane still gripped purposefully in hand. Earlier he'd promised himself a little light relief after the serious business was over - a little sport by way of revenge for the way in which she'd dared to expose herself to him wearing nothing below the waist apart from those minuscule see-through knickers. So he was hugely tempted to make a few cuts of the cane vertically across the welts that decorated her already. That would cause the very maximum pain and suffering, but it would also spoil the pretty pattern he'd taken such care to imprint upon her. The result would be aesthetically unpleasing, despite the intense satisfaction the strokes themselves would provide. So he'd proceed in the manner he'd originally intended. He'd lay a few strokes across the tops of her thighs... but there'd be a definite change of caning technique...

It was over, Jennie groaned to herself with relief. It was over at last. All the strokes had finally been laid across her poor backside. She was in agony, but at least there was no more to come. The pain would endure for ages, but at least no additional torture was going to be inflicted upon her. Somehow she'd come through it. Somehow she'd survived. Her rear was burning like a petrol-fed bonfire on November the fifth, but no more fuel was to be added to the flames. What must it look like? Her multi-striped bottom, she meant. What a picture of distress it must make.

But, as she'd just said to herself, at least the torment was over. At least it was all over and done. She supposed she'd better not try to stand up until Mr Stanley—

Thwack!

The cane sliced happily across the very tops of her thighs, making her throw back her head and shriek in surprise, despite Mr Stanley's earlier orders. Then she shrieked again, this time with her hands clamped over her mouth, as Mr Stanley branded her thighs thrice more in rapid succession. All four cuts partially overlapped the one before, thereby creating a corrugated welt effect just below each candy-striped cheek. The sea of white goose bumps could not disguise the bright, blood-red colour of the severely caned buttocks and thighs. There would be no perching on the edge of her typing stool in order to ease the discomfort, Mr Stanley told himself happily. The tops of her legs would be almost as painful as the prettily decorated bottom that blazed with pride less than half an inch above.

'Keep your hands over your mouth, Mrs Jamieson,' he warned, before adding a final two strokes to the recently raised thigh-welt.

Part Five

At long last Mr Stanley decided it was almost time for Jennie to return to an upright position. It was half an hour since the cane had last landed. Half an hour during which he'd left her bent over the back of the chair, the cane lying on the table beside her, until the sobbing turned to no more than laboured breathing. Half an hour during which he'd shuffled his paperwork and directed the occasional work-orientated question towards her, while all the time feasting his eyes on the glorious scenery a few short feet in front of his desk. He felt sure that making her stay in that pose, beaten and burning before him, had significantly heightened her distress. He was certain she'd found it just as humbling and humiliating as when he'd made her wait for the punishment to start. Possibly even more so.

He bided his time for a further five minutes before clearing his throat. 'Mrs Jamieson?' he said sharply, his gaze still glued to the mass of pulsating multi-welts that ran across her buttocks and upper thighs.

She didn't dare to turn her head or lift her forehead from the tabletop. 'Yes, Mr Stanley?' she whispered, as nervous as she'd ever felt in her life.

'Am I able to assume that there will be no repeat of last night's deplorable behaviour? No further incidents of copulation in the chemistry laboratory or, indeed, elsewhere?'

'Oh yes, Mr Stanley,' she replied without hesitation. 'I swear it'll never happen again. Never.'

'You'll know what to expect if it does?'

'It won't, Mr Stanley. It won't.'

'I'm to take it that the lesson has been learnt?'

'Oh yes, definitely, Mr Stanley. Most definitely learnt. I can assure you of that.'

'And it will be remembered, will it?'

'Yes, Mr Stanley, it will always be remembered. Always. I promise.'

'You don't think I should add another reminder or two right now?'

'No, no, not at all. Definitely not. There's absolutely no need for that at all.'

'Then kindly gather yourself together and fetch your notebook.'

She sighed with relief and then straightened up, slowly and very uncomfortably, teardrops still drying on her face. 'My notebook?' she asked, before glimpsing the cane and immediately averting her eyes, unable to tolerate the sight of the instrument that had caused her so much pain.

'Yes, if you please. Kindly collect your notebook. Now that this highly distasteful business has at long last been concluded there's work that has to be done.'

Very gingerly she ran the fingertips of both hands over her buttocks, and gasped in dismay. The swellings felt enormous! Particularly the one that ran across the middle of both cheeks. How many strokes had it taken to raise that? Oh, mother! It was just impossible to soothe herself with her hands. Rubbing them over her bottom only made matters worse. She was just so incredibly tender and sore.

She turned sideways to Mr Stanley and then stooped straight-legged to retrieve her clothes from the floor. 'Ouch,' she gasped, discovering too late that the retightening of the skin on her buttocks caused considerable extra discomfort.

Much to Mr Stanley's delight.

She placed her knickers on the writing table, well away from the cane. There was no way she was going to be able to wear those snug little things. Then she stepped into her skirt, drawing it gingerly up and wincing as it touched. It tightened across her bottom as she pulled up the zip, making her start. She must try her utmost not to show any more signs of distress, she told herself firmly. Now she was respectably covered up it was time to regain some composure. How awful it had been, having to carry on a conversation with Mr Stanley whilst bent over that chair. At least he could now talk to her face instead of the colourfully striped cheeks of her bare bottom.

With her knickers in hand she walked stiffly across the carpet towards her small adjoining room, holding her breath. Each step caused the lightweight material of the skirt to rub painfully against her. Oh! Ouch! Ow! She was in agony. Her bottom had never been so incredibly hot and sore. She'd been spanked before, of course, several times. Her poor posterior simply seemed to attract that sort of attention. But never had she suffered anything remotely like this. The lower half of her body was on fire. It throbbed and burned with a rage she'd never have believed possible.

She'd have to take the bus home from school, standing up. She couldn't possibly sit down to drive. She'd have to take the bus and make absolutely sure she was in bed in the spare room before Michael came home. In bed, face down, of course. In bed, face down, and suffering from a severe case of flu. A sudden and severe bout of flu that would last for several days. How awful that was going to be. How boring, as well as everything else.

Oh crumbs, as she walked out of the room she could just tell that Mr Stanley was staring in fascination at the tightly filled seat of her skirt, and relishing the thought of how he'd dealt so extensively with the bouncy bare bottom that wiggled from side to side underneath. She supposed she'd better get used to the idea that he'd be doing it every day he saw her from now on. Would anyone else at school be doing the same? She knew - only too well - how men talked. Suppose word somehow got out that she'd been caught with her knickers down in the chemistry lab and then caned by the headmaster for her sins? She'd never be able to live it down if that happened. She'd go red in the face whenever she had to leave the privacy of her room. Everywhere she went people would be gawping after her and speculating with intrigue on the way she'd had her bare bottom caned by her employer. She'd have to face that group of cheeky young lads in the upper sixth form who already called her 'Sweetarse' and made all sorts of other suggestive remarks. Remarks that she'd always found quite amusing and complimentary, up to now. Good grief, they hadn't even let her forget that she'd smooched with the ringleader, Slim Trelawny, at the school dance last Christmas, and allowed him to grope her bottom on the dance floor! 'Hello, Sweetarse,' Slim's pal, Tim Adams, had said the following morning. 'I hear your finest feature gave Slim an incredibly hard time last night. Come here and we'll see if it does the same thing to me!'

'Don't you dare!' she'd giggled, backing away from him just in case.

Many, many comments of a similar nature had been made over the course of the succeeding months. So what in God's name would they say to her if they ever discovered what had happened that morning?

Well at least there was one consolation. She'd had a beautiful bonk last night. A really beautiful bonk, despite the unfortunate ending. Mr Parker had been a red-hot lover, and she'd been able to position herself over the edge of the bench in such a way that each thrust from behind caused her clit to rub against the surface. However viciously she'd been caned, no one could take that memory away from her. Mind you, if she could turn back the clock she'd do so like a shot. Oh! Oh! Ouch! Her poor little, sore little bum!

She dropped the minuscule panties into a drawer, before cleaning her face with a wipe and applying some eye make-up. Then she slid a hand up the back of her short skirt, carefully checking her injured parts. Well, at least they were fully covered. The lowest throbbing thigh-welt was about an inch above the hem, so she'd be okay for the rest of the day, provided she remembered not to bend forward too far.

She returned to Mr Stanley, shorthand notebook and pencil in hand. 'Just turn off the air conditioning and put these files away first,' he said quietly, savouring the warm feeling of smug satisfaction as he watched those proudly pert buttocks undulating their way across the room. Their very painful way across the room. Never again would they be a source of frustration for him. Much, much the opposite, in fact. He'd always be able to recall every tiny detail of the way he'd scorched them into total submission. He'd always be able to visualise every blistering, raised welt. 'And file these timetables in the lower drawer of the cabinet,' he added, enjoying the thought of the way she'd be obliged to bend over in front of him once again.

She finished her tasks, studiously refusing to look at the cane that still lay across the mahogany table, and then stood in front of his desk.

'Please sit down, Mrs Jamieson.'

'I'd rather stand.'

'I realise that. Nevertheless, please sit down.'

She started to lower herself slowly and tentatively onto the chair, but immediately jerked to her feet with a squeal of pain. 'I can't do it,' she groaned. 'I simply can't sit down.'

He smiled happily. 'Very well, Mrs Jamieson, remain on your feet if you must.'

'Thank you.'

'Go and see Mr Parker,' he began. 'Tell him that his fourth form rugby practice has been cancelled. The caretaker's short-handed, so he's to clean the toilets instead. And then my car.'

'Yes, Headmaster.'

'Then speak to the caretaker. Explain to him that he is personally to supervise the cleansing of the bench in the chemistry lab that was the scene of last night's disgraceful misbehaviour on your part.'

She coloured but said nothing.

'Then report to Miss Stricton. She will need reassurance that last night's gross misconduct has been dealt with appropriately. She says that the horrifying experience in the chemistry lab will haunt her for the rest of her days. Particularly the disgusting spectacle of you wriggling your naked bottom in delight whilst Mr Parker ejaculated all over them.'

Part Six

Simon 'Slim' Trelawny sat in the sixth form common room, staring thoughtfully out of the window. He was aged seventeen, bordering on eighteen, and was the ringleader of the 'cheeky young lads' about whom Jennie had been pondering a while earlier. Slim was the one who'd danced with her at the Christmas disco, his hands all over her bottom and his dick jammed solidly into her stomach. Those ten minutes or so on the dance floor had lived in his memory ever since. He could still feel the creamy-smooth texture of her buttocks through the thin material of her evening gown. He could still recall the way she squealed and giggled when he squeezed them hard with both hands, and how she then responded by wriggling her groin against the mega-stiffness of his own.

And now, Slim mused to himself, it seemed that the unimaginable just might become the attainable. It seemed that the impossible dream of porking the posterior off their unbelievably fuckable school secretary might not be quite as impossible as it had always appeared...

Earlier that morning he'd been sauntering along the little-used pathway that led through the shrub garden and past the offices of the headmaster and school secretary. Jennie's window was wide open and he poked his head inside, hoping she'd be at her desk. 'Hello, Sweetarse,' he was going to say. 'Don't forget that I know exactly what it is you're sitting on.' The room had been empty, but he heard Mr Stanley speaking - out of sight in his adjoining office.

'These parts have sinned!' Mr Stanley exclaimed. 'Not only have they sinned against the trust and authority that others have placed in me, but they have also sinned against your lawful wedded husband. They have failed disgracefully in their duty to keep themselves only unto him. But fear not, I shall grant them absolution. I shall purify them with fire! I shall purify them with a fire so intense that they'll think twice before ever sinning again!'

There'd come a loud crack like a rifle shot, followed by a shriek of pain.

'Be silent, Mrs Jamieson,' he heard Mr Stanley say angrily. 'Do you want the whole school to know that your bare bottom is being caned for the way it was found fornicating on school premises last night?'

For more than sixty minutes Slim stood outside that open window listening with intrigue... and then intent...

Slim's pals, the other 'cheeky young lads', Tim and Baby Jim, sat in front of him, their minds boggling with the prospect of the proposals he'd just finished outlining to them.

'You're quite sure of what you heard?' asked Jim.

'Completely. Every word was as clear as could be. Not to mention the crack of the cane and the cries of despair.'

'Fucked by Mr Parker? Last night? In the chemistry lab?'

'Yep.'

'And then caned by Mr Stanley this morning?'

'Yep.'

'Brilliant!' enthused Tim. 'Absolutely brilliant, Slim!'

Miss Stricton stared down intently for a full sixty seconds. Then at last she spoke. 'Yes, I think I can agree that Mr Stanley has executed his highly unpalatable duty with all due diligence.'

'That's good...'

'But only so far as it goes.'

'Pardon?'

'Am I correct in thinking that there has been no application of the hand on here... or here?'

'That's right...'

'No spanking at all? Neither before nor after the caning?'

'Erm, no...'

'An unfortunate oversight, but one I can remedy soon enough. Hold still, young lady. Hold very still indeed.'

'No, please don't...'

As the lunch break approached its end, Slim rose purposefully to his feet. 'Here she comes now,' he murmured happily, 'crossing the quadrangle towards us. Rather slowly and stiffly, it seems to me. Come on you lucky buggers; let's confront her with our requirements for the afternoon. Leave me to do all the talking.'

'What time does my husband get home tonight?' Jennie echoed in surprise, staring at Slim Trelawny and grappling with her mind to follow the reasoning behind the question. 'Why on earth do you want to know that?'

'We're concerned for your welfare, Mrs Jamieson. We're anxious to help you all we can.'

'I don't understand...'

Slim stared keenly into her eyes. 'We would like to spend the afternoon explaining to you, by way of reassurance, that it would never once cross our minds to tell your husband about what happened to you this morning in the headmaster's study. We want to spend the whole afternoon, all three of us, explaining to you how we would never dream of phoning him at work and letting the proverbial cat out of the bag. We want to spend the entire afternoon - and some of the evening too - making absolutely sure you appreciate our concern about this matter. We want to spend as much time as we can with you today, so you'll be totally confident that he'll never hear of it from us. We want to ram the point home to you as forcefully as possible, time after time, so you won't feel troubled about this particularly worrying problem ever again. I'm sure you follow my meaning?'

Jennie stared back at him and then at the others, seeing the lust shining brightly in their eyes. She understood only too well. There was no mistaking their intent. 'Oh, my God,' she groaned at length.

'You can drive us back to your house now if you like, Mrs Jamieson. We'll skip lessons for the rest of the day. It will give us that extra bit of time in which to banish your fears.'

'Perhaps you'll do one thing for me?' she gulped. 'If you want me to drive you, I mean...'

'And what's that?'

'If you want me to drive you, one of you will have to go to the common room and find me the largest, softest cushion you can.'

Baby Jim sat in the back of the car with Tim. Although seventeen he was known as Baby Jim because of his fresh, open face that made him appear several years younger. And he had the manners and politeness to go with it. He was by no means sure he should be doing what he was doing. He liked Mrs Jamieson. He liked her a lot. Not just in the way that Slim and Tim liked her. Not just because he wanted to get inside her knickers. He liked her as a person. They'd often chatted briefly, and he'd gained the impression that she also liked him. But what would she think of him now? What would she think of the way he was allowing Slim to blackmail her into pleasuring the three of them? Surely she'd feel nothing but dislike and contempt. But, however unfortunate that might be, he supposed that nothing and no one was capable of stopping him taking advantage of her that afternoon. Nothing and no one. However much he liked her as a person, nothing was going to stop him having his evil way with her, even though he was well aware it was wrong. Even though he was ashamed - very ashamed - of what he was about to do. Or rather, of what he hoped he was about to do. But hate himself as he might well later, if there was going to be a chance of getting his end away with her he was going to grasp it with both hands. The chance, he meant, of course. Not his end...

But surely Slim's idea would never work out? Surely there was no way in the world that this absolutely ravishing, respectably married woman was going to let the three of them spend the entire afternoon fucking her for all they were worth? Surely there wasn't?

But Jennie realised there was. Not only that there was, but also that she had no real alternative. Just a couple of words to her husband and she'd be dropped in the proverbial right up to her ears. She had no choice in the matter. If the three of them were determined to take advantage of her vulnerability, then take advantage they certainly would. There was nothing she could do to prevent it. Nothing whatsoever.

Jennie winced and gasped as the car ran over a small rut in the road surface - the flash of pain reminiscent of a stroke from the cane. But somehow her rear was becoming inured to its painful condition and she was able to prevent herself crying out loud at the discomfort. She'd never have believed it possible. A short while ago she'd never have believed she'd be able to sit in her car, with or without such a wonderfully plump cushion. She'd never have believed it possible to bear any pressure at all for days. It must be, like everything else, that she was simply getting used to it. That she was getting used to the torture Mr Stanley had inflicted on her poor, undeserving behind...

Ouch! Not that used to it, unfortunately. She'd better slow down even more; she didn't want to hit another bump the size of that one at that sort of speed again.

It was incredible, she thought. It was incredible, but true. Her rear had been flayed alive, yet her wretchedly wayward pussy was also on fire. Once again. She was as moist as could be, and she knew it had more than a little to do with the way she'd been punished. Her body had reacted to the outrageously fierce treatment in just the same way as it had to the much lighter spankings she'd had in the past. The pain from which she was suffering had, somehow, turned her on - for the second time since Mr Stanley had started to wield the cane. It was making her really horny. It was making her long to have her lovely Michael

41

slotted deep inside...

Ouch! Another irregularity in the road. Another flash of pain that made her even hotter and wetter than ever...

Slim, Tim, and despite himself, Baby Jim, had one thought in mind, and one thought only - the buried treasure they hoped and prayed was lying in wait for them at the junction of the school secretary's long, shapely legs. The hot little hole of the married woman behind the wheel of the car. All of them had done it a couple of times before, but only with inexperienced girls. Only in their wildest dreams had they done it with a married woman some ten years older.

Baby Jim felt another twinge of guilty conscience, and tried to put it to one side. He mustn't allow the other two to gain an inkling of how he felt. Neither of them would understand. Slim was such a real bugger that he wouldn't give a moment's thought to the rights and wrongs of the current situation. And Tim was so thick-skinned that the point wouldn't even occur to him. He'd just follow Slim's lead, as always.

Jim sighed silently. Anyway, why should he let it bother him in this way? Why should he feel bad about taking advantage of things? After all, she'd been caught on the job with Mr Parker. She'd been caught having it off in the chemistry lab. But even so...

Slim reached out and placed a hand on Jennie's bare, nicely rounded knee. 'Are you sitting comfortably?' he asked with a grin.

She wriggled her hips involuntarily. 'Not exactly.'

'Is there far to go?'

'Just down here,' she replied, flinching as she turned the car into a wide road lined with chestnut trees and then hit another bump. 'Ouch, that hurts.'

'We should have taken a bus,' Jim murmured from the back seat. 'Then you could've stood up. That would've been much more comfortable for you.'

Mr Stanley sat at his desk, deep in thought. What a spellbinding morning it had proven. An experience to savour forever. How he relished the memory. Particularly the stark contrast between the before and after. First the sight of those bare buttocks gleaming up at him, untouched and creamy-white, shameless in their beauty and perfection. Proud and impudent in the extreme. Perfectly sculpted cheeks, honey-smooth and saucily dimpled, pouting nervously up at him as they awaited the torment that lay ahead. And later - when he finally placed the cane back on the table beside her - what a picture she made. How could he possibly describe it? How could he ever put into words the intensity of the gratification he'd felt at the way those majestically proud buttocks had been so thoroughly transformed? So completely and utterly altered. By doing that to her he'd 'had' her far more comprehensively than he could in any other way. He had her and possessed her in the very truest sense. In a far, far truer way than Mr Parker had her the night before. He'd humbled her and hurt her and subjugated her whole being to his will. That was the ultimate in sexual achievement. That was what every man was attempting, but failing, to achieve during the act of carnal knowledge. Total domination...

And the protests of pain she'd been unable to totally contain. What music to his ears! And coupled to that, the sight of each freshly raised welt...

The cane had risen and fallen so effortlessly. Yet within the merest fraction of a second flawless flesh was wondrously blistered and burnt in a long thick line of excruciating torture. Thirteen times he'd disciplined her in this way, producing the same glorious result with every downward stroke. The same instantaneous blistering and sobs. The same ugly red welt and the same wails of outrage. Thirteen times he laid the fire across her buttocks, gaining the same transcendental joy each time. Thirteen times he sliced that cheating little bottom into sections, exactly as it deserved. Thirteen times he vented his anger for the way it had tormented him so greatly in the past. For the way it had mocked him and held him in such contempt. Could anything, anywhere, ever be so sweet?

Jennie eased herself out of the car and gasped with relief. Standing in the large gravel driveway of her house, she surveyed the three young men. 'You're serious about this?' she asked at last.

'Absolutely,' replied Slim. 'We feel you need all the comfort and reassurance we can possibly give you. And then maybe some more on top. We want to convince you how well we understand the fact that your good husband must never hear a word of what's transpired today. We want you to know how aware we are of the disastrous effect it would have upon your marriage.'

She was unable to prevent herself lowering her gaze to the fronts of their trousers. Three bulging, stretched fronts that told the whole sad tale only too well. She gulped and glanced, red-faced, at her watch. 'In that case I'd better phone mother and arrange for her to hang on to the boys after she collects them from school,' she sighed, reaching into her handbag for her mobile.

They followed her into the house, eyes riveted in fascination to the outline of unknickered buttocks clearly discernible through the seat of her short blue skirt. When they thought about what lay hidden from view under there...!

Jennie could feel their gaze all over her bottom. It seemed to make her burn even more - in the region of her wounded flesh as well as deep inside her loins. 'Would you like something to drink?' she asked, when they were in the living room. The boys declined, but she poured herself a stiff vodka and orange and downed it in two deep draughts. Then she poured herself another and despatched it in much the same way. 'So you're expecting to have sex with me, are you?' she asked, replacing her glass on top of the drinks cabinet. 'All three of you, is that right?'

Jim dropped his eyes to the floor and shuffled his feet. Tim looked sideways at Slim. 'We rather thought we might,' drawled that worthy, looking as cool as an ice-cube at the Arctic. 'Shall we all go upstairs and see what comes up?'

It had already come up, Baby Jim thought as she led the way up to the master bedroom. Very powerfully indeed...

While she climbed the stairs in front of them, all three cocked their heads to one side, gazing in appreciation at the view just above. 'No knickers,' mused

Slim, having reached out and flicked up the hem of her skirt, thereby affording them the very briefest glimpse of sorely welted buttocks. 'Surely you haven't been anticipating our visit?'

Jennie looked back at him over her shoulder. 'They're too tight and uncomfortable,' she informed him. 'If you know what I mean.'

'We've seen part of what you mean for ourselves,' he chortled. 'But knickerless girls really shouldn't wear short skirts, you know. Not when they're climbing the stairs ahead of three horny young men. I don't think your husband would approve.'

She walked into the bedroom, defiantly swishing her hips and then catching her breath at the sudden discomfort. 'He likes me wearing short skirts,' she responded, tossing her hair. 'With or without knickers.'

Slim was not to be outdone. 'Any girl who looks good in a miniskirt looks even better out of it, as I think you're soon going to prove.'

She stood in the middle of the large master bedroom, facing them, knowing she had little or no choice in the matter. Knowing she was no longer the mistress of her own destiny. If these three young studs were going to insist on having her each in turn, then by each in turn she was going to be had. There was no doubting that fact. She didn't dare to call their bluff, even though they probably wouldn't phone Michael and tell him about the caning. She simply couldn't take that risk. If they really were intent on having their way with her, then she'd just have to go along with their wishes. At least her lack of say in the matter would help ease her conscience when they were through.

Again Jennie looked down at the bursting trouser fronts. Good grief, they seemed to be more than doubly endowed! Surely she was wrong...

Silence reigned for almost a minute, during which time she wondered just how they'd proceed. Maybe they'd lose their nerve, she reflected, but on the other hand it seemed far more likely that she'd lose her virtue instead. Several times over, judging by the determination they'd shown up to now. She had to say she was a little bit disappointed in Baby Jim. She'd always thought of him as such a nice, straightforward young lad. But could she really blame him? Could she blame him for following Slim? How many nice, straightforward young lads would decline such an opportunity when offered on a plate? Not very many, she felt sure. If the truth were told it was only natural that he should put his finer feelings to one side and grab whatever slice of the action he could. Whatever slice he could grab of her lacerated rear...

'I have it on the best authority that you've been caned by the headmaster,' Slim stated at last.

'I thought you'd already seen some of the marks.'

'Only a very quick flash. We'd like to have a much longer look at them all.'

'Would you indeed?' she challenged, looking him straight in the eye, but he held her gaze with calm composure.

'We would,' he replied after a pause, returning her stare. 'Very much so. Over there in the full light from the window, if you'd be so kind.'

Jennie stood with her back to the boys, bathed in bright sunlight, shoulders back and proudly defiant, her hands gripping the hem of her skirt, a graceful picture of nubile femininity at its best. She had nothing to be ashamed about, she told herself once again. This was none of her seeking, after all.

'Come on, my lovely,' urged Slim. 'Your audience is growing restless.'

'Give her a little more time,' urged Baby Jim.

'Thank you,' she said to him over her shoulder, 'you're very kind.'

'But I'm not,' growled Slim, 'and neither is Tim. We want to see exactly what you have there under your skirt. And we want to see it now, don't we, Tim?'

'Too right, matey!' Tim agreed enthusiastically, trying to adjust his tightly stretched trouser front. 'I'm bursting to see, quite literally.'

'She's nervous,' Jim persisted. 'Be a bit more patient.'

'I'm okay, Jim,' she said softly.

'You don't have much alternative,' laughed Slim.

'You're quite right,' she agreed ruefully.

'Come on, then, let's all have an eyeful of what you've got hidden away. Let's see what Mr Stanley's done to your lovely bum.'

She took a deep breath and, blushing fiercely, lifted the hem until the skirt was above her waist, and three sharp, rasping intakes of breath were followed by absolute silence as the young men goggled in wide-eyed disbelief at the gorgeous bottom so brutally beaten. The valley between each prettily dimpled cheek was deep, and the cheeks themselves resembled an inverted heart. They were plump yet firm and pert, full and rounded at the bottom, then tapering upwards in perfect proportions as far as the small of her back. And they were decorated so appealingly by Mr Stanley's cane that each of the young men felt in imminent danger of coming to the boil there and then. There and then as he stood gaping, open-mouthed, at the spectacular swell of her wickedly caned buttocks and upper thighs. While they stood there staring - spellbound and rooted to the spot - each felt his already overgrown erection pushing even further up the flat of his stomach as it stretched and strained at the leash. Although none of them quite knew why, the beauty of her naked bottom was significantly enhanced by the swellings and fiery red lines across it. The red and white raised welts emphasised the graceful curves and hollows in a way they found impossible to understand.

For long minutes they stood gawping, while Jennie was getting wetter and wetter thanks to the way she could actually feel their gaze upon her.

Then, still speechless, Slim moved forward and, very lightly, cupped each grievously stricken orb. She closed her eyes and held her breath in apprehension, but he was so gentle with her that she felt her insides melt. He could feel the heat from the caning against each palm. It seemed impossible that she could be so fiercely ablaze. At length he found his voice. 'How on earth did you manage to drive?' he croaked.

'I suppose you get used to it after a while.'

'You need some cold cream,' suggested Jim.

'That's a great idea,' agreed Slim, regaining much of his previous self-assurance. 'Do you have some?'

'In the cabinet,' she replied, nodding towards the en-suite bathroom.

'Get it, Jim,' said Slim, then moved her forward and bent her over the dressing table until she was resting, straight legged, on her elbows. Slowly and tenderly he applied the cream, making her gasp and then moan with the delicious relief it brought. Briefly his fingertips slid inside her two lower openings, turning the moans to groans of delight. Then he was back to his ministrations, soothing and salving each cruel cut. 'Oh, that's so good...' she whispered, shivering with pleasure at the way she was being so pampered and petted. On worked Slim, massaging cream into burning flesh. 'Oh...' she gasped again, 'that's really, really nice...'

Eventually Slim stepped back and eased her into an upright stance. 'Now then,' he murmured, 'Tim and Jim will help you out of your clothes while I kick off my own kit.'

Willingly, the two lads stripped her down to her high heels. It took Tim only a matter of seconds to unzip and remove her skirt, whereas Baby Jim's untutored fingers fumbled inexpertly with blouse and bra. But at last the catch at the front of her bra was unclipped and full, firm breasts tumbled warmly into his hands, tipped with pointed nipples that pressed into his palms as he squeezed.

While Tim and Jim pawed her, gently but thoroughly, Jennie turned her head and looked over her shoulder at the naked Slim. She was shocked by the awesome brutality of his penis. It reached up past his navel, long and thick, and with a distinctly purplish hue. It was the biggest she'd seen in thirteen years of sexual encounters, both in length and girth. A great horn of rock hard flesh standing stiffly to attention in anticipation of all she had to offer. A huge swathe of iron-hard brawn that made her stomach churn with apprehension. And his balls were exactly in keeping - large and hanging heavy with male seed. She squeezed her thighs together and started a mini-orgasm just at the sight. She'd never felt more turned on. She'd never felt so vulnerable, yet so deliciously ready for what was to come...

Tim and Jim were out of their clothes, and unashamedly she studied their tackle. They were almost in the same league as Slim. She swallowed hard and tried to control her feelings. It really wouldn't be right to let them perceive how worked up she'd become; no respectably married young wife and mother should be reacting to her unfortunate plight in this way.

She turned to face the three of them, proud in the knowledge that they'd appreciate her body. And appreciate it they certainly did. They gawped hungrily at her outthrust breasts, slim waist, and shaven sex. 'Bloody hell!' Slim breathed in awe.

She dropped her eyes, once again, to his rampant mid-section. 'Ditto...' she said, but only to herself.

'You're beautiful,' groaned Baby Jim, barely able to formulate the words. 'Really, really beautiful.'

'Thank you,' she whispered, smiling at him briefly but warmly.

Imagine waking up every morning beside that lovely bare pussy, Slim thought. Not to mention those boobs and that bum. That fabulous bare bum that made you want to clamp your hands right round it and crush the smooth flesh between your fingers. What sort of man was her husband? What sort of man was he to deserve such treasures?

For another minute or so they stood staring at each other: Jennie at the row of pulsing male organs that confronted her so menacingly, the youths at the vision of delight that nestled so nicely between the very tops of her thighs. She shivered. It seemed she might be about to disprove the mathematical proposition that three into one won't go. She'd never seen three such upright, upstanding young men. Thank heavens Michael wasn't hung in the same way; she'd never be able to cope with it day after day after day...

Oh crumbs! Three seventeen-year-old lads with raging hormones and hard-ons! Think of the strength and stamina they'd possess between them! Think of the combined yardage they were going to be able to pump into her over the course of the next few hours! It was beginning to look as if her own resources were about to be stretched to the very fullest of their full capacity. Maybe even beyond...

Slim took a confident step forward. 'So then,' he said quietly, 'the moment of truth is upon us.'

Slim turned her around, before sitting on a dressing chair and then drawing her very sore, very bare bottom slowly and carefully down onto his knee. The two others sat on the bed facing them, eagerly waiting for events to unfold right in front of their eyes. Slim could feel the fearsome heat of the caning against the sensitive skin of his lap. He drew her hair to one side and kissed the nape of her neck. 'Is this too uncomfortable?' he had the decency to whisper, half turning her face towards his own with his right hand. She shook her head and he kissed her deeply with his tongue, making her even wetter. She wriggled her hips very slightly and gasped with pleasure at the sharp stab of pain it produced. So she wriggled and gasped even more. Never would she have believed such a thing possible. Never would she have believed her body could respond in this way. So with his tongue still in her mouth she wriggled harder than ever against him, experiencing even more of the same delight. Of course she knew from past experience that a hotly spanked bottom always made her feel extra feminine and sexy, but this was quite different. This time she was actually enjoying the intense pain - enjoying, for its own sake, the severe streak of fire that branded her. It produced a sort of mini-orgasm each time. It was much more exciting than just a warmly glowing backside making her feel a bit randier than usual. In fact, it was one of the most delicious sensations she'd ever known. Despite herself she was now yearning impatiently for what she knew lay in store for her that afternoon, and how much longer would she be able to keep that highly disreputable fact to herself...?

Slim broke the kiss and began nibbling the back of her neck, his left hand cupping her magnificent breasts. She sighed and parted her legs to allow his other hand to explore. He bit her neck very softly. 'Our friend was right,' he murmured, nodding towards Jim, while feeling her juices hot and sticky against his fingertips. 'You are incredibly beautiful.' His fingers began stroking and teasing each swollen nipple in turn.

'You're being very gentle with me,' she whispered contentedly, but Slim knew it was very easy for someone in her situation to speak too soon.

She pressed her buttocks firmly against the heat and power of his erection and started to moan. Slowly he sank two fingers into the glorious wet warmth that lay open between her thighs. It was impossibly easy for him to use his fingers in her. Her insides were on fire and as oily as anyone could wish. She was so open and slick that he seemed to slide into her without any pressure from him, just as if she'd drawn him in of her own accord. Within seconds he was inside her up to the knuckles, the front and back of his hand wet. Then he started to use his thumb to massage her clitoris, her response immediate as sweetly and tenderly she began to climax, groaning and wriggling her hips slowly and dreamily in synchronisation with the push and pull of his fingers.

Slim was amazed at the internal heat she was generating. He'd never imagined that anyone could be so hot. 'You're enjoying this after all?' he asked unnecessarily.

'Mmmmm...' she confirmed, eyes tightly shut.

Tim and Jim stared at Slim's fingers working slowly in and out. 'So are we,' added Tim.

Once again she felt her insides starting to spasm against the trespassing fingers. 'Jesus!' Baby Jim muttered under his breath, his eyes riveted to the delightful sight of wet pussy being delicately but thoroughly probed. She opened her eyes and looked into his face. Despite the distraction posed by Slim she managed a watery smile. Then she closed her eyes and started to moan with desire. She was falling headlong into the abyss. The dark, delightful abyss she knew only too well. And the fact that she was being fingered in full view of the two friends only served to heighten the excitement she felt. Somehow she liked the idea of Tim and Baby Jim watching intently as Slim's glistening fingers glided smoothly back and forth.

She'd open her eyes and smile at Jim again in a minute, she decided. She wanted to be able to look right into his eyes at the same time as she could feel Slim working away between her legs. She wanted Jim to see her reactions. She wanted him to understand the way in which she was being aroused. She wanted him to see and understand all that, as well as to watch Slim's fingers at work inside her.

Carefully Slim extracted himself from her and looked up at Tim. 'Your turn,' he murmured, slowly rubbing the oil on his fingers into her nipples. 'There's plenty to go round.'

Tim needed no further bidding. He knelt on the floor to her right and eagerly reached out. She gasped as he pushed his fingers into boiling syrup, much more roughly than Slim had done. 'Christ, she's on fire!' he said in surprise. 'She's as hot as hell itself!'

'I know what you mean,' agreed Slim.

'Ahhh...' she sighed, writhing in appreciation as Tim started to dip and delve and Slim continued to massage bare nipples and breasts. She spread her legs even wider and then looked over at Jim. He sensed her eyes on him and lifted his gaze from her crotch. He smiled shyly into her fever-bright eyes. She was now too hot and bothered to respond in kind, but he thought he could detect a hint of a smile behind her wide-eyed stare. Jim realised that slowly but surely his friends were bringing her off yet again, and he also realised she was enjoying him gazing into her face as they did so. Her flushed, sweetly contorted face.

Jennie came with a sudden rush, much more fiercely than before, sobbing and groaning loudly as she shuddered on Slim's lap, rolling her head from side to side as her climax hammered right through her. Tim's fingers stayed deep inside, prompting and provoking her to even greater heights of desire. And Jim continued to gape in fascination. Never before had he seen a girl so sexually responsive.

At last she was through. At last her orgasm receded, leaving her breathless and exhausted. Tim withdrew his fingers and stood up. For several seconds Jim gazed at her glistening sex lips. He sighed to himself. It would be a long while before he'd be able to introduce himself into there. Slim would undoubtedly go first, leaving Tim to follow and Jim a long, sticky way third. But he could wait. He could wait a lifetime and a half if it meant collecting such a mind-boggling prize as that sweet little hole...

Slim bent her across the dressing table until she was in her earlier pose, shapely caned bottom on prominent display. She was more than ready, she sighed to herself. Dreadful though it was to admit, at that particular moment she wanted nothing more than Slim's colossus inside her. She was more ready for it than she'd ever been in her life. The cane, and all that had followed, ensured that fact. 'Oh!' she gasped, opening her mouth and closing her eyes as she felt the tip of his mammoth appendage begin to nose its powerful way inside. 'Oh, that's good!'

And it certainly was. It was so good it almost hurt. Slim had taken a firm grip around her waist and was forcing himself, very slowly, deeper and deeper inside. She gasped again at the heat and the girth of the weapon sinking into her. He paused to savour the moment and she could feel how huge he was, even though he was only halfway in.

At last she could feel him starting to move forward again. She screwed up her eyes and held her breath as he began to force-feed himself to her, as he began a deeper and deeper invasion into the soft, yielding privacy of her person.

Deeper and deeper he sank, on and on, penetrating her to what seemed an impossible degree. She groaned inwardly. How much more did he have left at his disposal? She was already incredibly full. She was already extremely replete...

Relentlessly he pressed on, packing her to capacity and beyond, bringing tears to her eyes as he stared down at her beautiful, welted buttocks and forced his way home in between. She opened her mouth to moan, but found she had to struggle for breath instead. And still there was more of him waiting - more of him still to enter.

She didn't dare move or wriggle against him. She just stood still waiting for him to finish impaling her with his brawn. And eventually he was all the way home. Home but far from dry. At last he was plugged in her right to the hilt - wedged into her as far as he could go.

So there she stood, motionless and straight legged, gasping for breath, her forehead and elbows resting on the table, her smooth round bottom several inches higher and pressed warmly into Slim's groin. Together the two of them shared the heat that the cane had laid across that lovely rear.

'Cinderella,' breathed Slim, 'at last I've found you. It fits!'

But only just, she gulped to herself with a wince. He was so deeply and rigidly embedded that she doubted whether she'd be able to straighten up without his cooperation. She was so thoroughly skewered she could feel herself fainting away - fainting headlong into oblivion. Her strength was just ebbing away. She was impaled and imprisoned upon him, and too weak even to raise her head. The glorious giant dick wedged so tightly inside her was draining all her vitality away.

Jennie began to moan softly, her eyes shut and her arms and cheek resting on the dressing table as if it were a pillow on which she was fast asleep. She could hear Tim saying something to her. She opened her mouth to reply, but was simply unable to formulate the words. 'Ooohhhh...' she groaned instead.

'I think you might have scored there,' Tim said to Slim. 'I think she's rather impressed.'

Slim plugged himself even further inside by pushing hard against the bouncy roundness of her buttocks. 'I must admit that I do seem to have made a pretty good connection,' he grunted. 'I hope you can agree, Mrs Jamieson?'

'Ahhh...' she slowly gasped, enjoying the thought that Baby Jim would be able to see exactly the effect his friend's enormous cock was having on her.

Slowly Slim began to fuck her, using long, even strokes of great power and weight, and the effect was immediate. Suddenly, around his rigid intrusion into her person, he could feel her starting to orgasm. He could feel her stretched insides starting to contract in a series of violent convulsions. Solid though he was, he could actually feel himself being compressed. She looked wide-eyed ahead of her, helpless and unseeing, her face flushed, teardrops slowly running down both cheeks and beads of perspiration standing out on her forehead. Her mouth was open, as if she was about to scream, but the only sound to emerge was that of her heavily laboured breathing. Her climax went on and on, silent but so intense that he actually began to worry.

But at last she began to groan. A long, low groan of contentment and relief. Then visibly she began to relax. 'Welcome back to the land of the living,' he said when he gauged she could hear him.

She giggled sexily and wriggled her bum against his groin. He began to withdraw, slowly and stickily. 'Your turn, Tim,' he murmured as he pulled out into the relative cold of the bedroom. 'You and Jim can have a quick dip if you like, before I start on her for real.'

Tim needed no further bidding. He was mounted on her buttocks and sliding deep inside her in less time than it takes to tell. 'Oh!' she gasped as he sank right to the hilt. 'Oh mother!' she gasped again, as he started to pump her with all his might.

'Just make sure you don't spunk in her,' Slim warned. 'I want to be the first to do that. Then afterwards we can all cream her as much as we like.'

Tim stopped and pulled out with a slurp, reluctant to yield but knowing he couldn't trust himself to abide by Slim's demand if he remained in situ much longer. He stared down at his gleaming wet cock. At least he'd been all the way inside her. Now all he had to do was be patient until Jim had briefly sampled her wares, and Slim had then given her all he possessed.

'Your go, Jim,' ordered Slim.

Jennie closed her eyes and sighed with pleasure as Jim sank slowly and tenderly in from behind, one hand cupped warmly round each breast as she remained bent forward across the dressing table. She liked him a lot more than his two friends. He was much more gentle and understanding. Considerate, almost. Yes, it was true, she really quite fancied him, she supposed. And disgraceful though it was, she had to admit that she'd been looking forward to this moment ever since she'd become aware of the dastardly nature of their intent. Having him inside her was much nicer than accommodating either of the other two. It was a bit like making love to a regular boyfriend, or husband.

'I love you,' he whispered into her ear, so softly that she only just caught what he said. But she pushed back with her bottom to let him know she'd heard, and then clenched him as tightly as she could with her vaginal muscles.

'You're gorgeous,' he breathed as the coitus got slowly and sweetly underway.

But it was over far too soon. On Slim's orders Jim had to backtrack all the way, leaving his glistening tool pointing rigidly up at the ceiling, aching painfully with frustrated desire. 'That was nice,' she said softly, smiling back at him over her shoulder.

'Yes it was,' he agreed with feeling, staring down at her sadistically striped bottom with a longing he'd never experienced before.

Slim wrapped his arms around her and picked her up like a baby. 'Now then, Mrs Jamieson,' he growled, taking purposeful steps towards the double bed, 'for the girl with the world's most spectacular body, the world's most spectacular fucking!'

Ten minutes later the scene in the matrimonial bedroom was as follows: whilst Tim and Baby Jim gaped in awe, Slim was mounted securely on Jennie's back as she lay face-down on the bed, his legs astride hers, fucking her slowly but very deliberately. He was forcing his stomach and groin deep into the blazing hot cheeks of her upturned bottom, in order to penetrate her to the full. Then he was easing back and lifting his groin, staring at the severely caned buttocks as his penis temporarily exited. After a pause he would sink back inside her again, very slowly, half an inch at a time, making her wait as long as he could, making her wait for the final push home. He was enjoying the way she wriggled and gasped in anticipation of receiving all he owned. And then, when he was all the way home, he was savouring the feel of a hot, silky-smooth bottom jammed hard against his stomach and groin, and of the tight channel he was skewering as far as it would stretch. Then he would start another retreat, just as slowly as before, feeling her insides tugging at him as he went, sensing their reluctance to yield any part of him up.

'At this rate we'll be here all night,' Tim complained Jim, anxious to begin his turn.

'There are worse ways of passing the time,' muttered Slim, withdrawing his tip into the relative cool of the air, and once again glancing down to admire the contours of her exquisitely shaped buttocks as she lay there, momentarily abandoned, awaiting further use. Then he bore down gradually, settling back inside her, watching his oversized organ disappear slowly between her wounded cheeks. 'Ohhh,' she moaned again as he stretched her further than she'd comfortably go.

Baby Jim wrapped both hands round his own unattended erection and sighed deeply, knowing he'd have to wait even longer than Tim.

Jennie groaned with pleasure at the way she was being extended. She still hadn't got used to Slim's dimensions, despite the time he'd already spent inside her. She supposed it had something to do with the way he was vacating her completely, and then waiting before starting all over again. Every time he returned she was surprised by his size. Surprised and highly delighted, she had to admit that. There was no way she could control how she felt. Oh dear, what a disgrace. What a positive and utter disgrace! Here she was, lying full stretch on the marital bed and wallowing in the pleasure of being comprehensively fucked by one of the sixth formers from school.

Tim strolled over to the bed for a closer inspection, just as Slim changed tactics. Having withdrawn and then waited, he suddenly shafted her as hard as he could - right to the root in barely a microsecond. Caught unaware she jerked back her head and squealed up at the ceiling in shocked surprise.

'Do that again,' Tim suggested from the side of the bed, so Slim did, producing exactly the same result. 'That's much more like it!' Tim enthused. He was hoping that a little increased activity would help speed his friend on his way. 'Doesn't she sound nice,' he rambled, as Jennie lifted her head and squealed yet again.

Slim had to agree, his excitement mounting, the pauses between each stroke getting shorter and shorter. Eventually there were no pauses at all and he was dishing out one long, continuous pounding, rutting in and out with force and speed. Jennie opened her mouth and groaned with delight at the way she was being so brutally plumbed and expanded, and the repeated flashes of pain across her welted bottom only served to heighten that delight, making her wish Mr Stanley had added a few more cuts before he'd allowed her to stand up...

Tim stayed on his feet by the bed. Not long now, he thought as Slim swept into overdrive.

But he'd misjudged the strength and determination of his friend. The assault and battery continued without any relent or respite. Ten, fifteen, twenty minutes slipped by, to the sound of rapid machine-gun fire as groin smacked hard against ultra-sore buttocks at a truly remarkable pace, accompanied by the slurping of penis in pussy, and the squeals of an overwrought young housewife in the throes of sexual abandon.

'The bugger will wear her away,' Tim grumbled to Jim. 'There'll be nothing left for us.'

Jim peered closely at Jennie, at the ecstatic look on her face. He stared at her upturned bottom, at the way it bounced so fetchingly under the barrage from above, and at the way Slim's long wet cock vanished between the bright red oval cheeks, only to appear a split second later and then vanish again. The glistening organ seemed to be gaining colour with every thrust; its fat, bulbous head seemed to be swelling with every plunge.

Jim told himself that when his time came he'd make love to her, as opposed to simply having sex. After all, he'd been desperately in love with her ever since she'd first appeared at school a year and a half ago, when he'd just turned sixteen...

Slim withdrew and paused for breath, just momentarily. He glanced down and was fascinated to see that her colourfully striped buttocks were now an even more fiery shade of red. Undoubtedly due to the ferocity of their fuck, he thought with pride. But unfortunately for him this sight and thought were very much his undoing, for he was struck with the sudden realisation that he couldn't hold back any longer. There was nothing he could do to avoid it. Matters had come to a head much sooner than he'd have wished...

Slim reacted swiftly, not wishing to waste a drop of the very special token of appreciation he'd been yearning to give to their school secretary ever since the Christmas dance.

Fortunately she was so open and ready for him that full re-entry was achieved just in time. As he sank back inside the wet warmth he closed his eyes and, with a groan, started to spurt. Jennie felt the first burst of piping hot seed and her climax started all over again. With each fresh squirt her vagina tightened greedily around him, as if trying to milk every last drop. She lifted her bottom and jammed it forcefully into his groin, determined that he should implant her as deeply as possible. Slim immediately reciprocated in kind, so as a result of their joint efforts he was embedded in her to his absolute maximum. No matter how much they wriggled and pushed against each other there was simply no more cock to go in. Which was probably just as well, she thought; bearing in mind how tightly he was fitted within.

And still he continued to ejaculate. 'Oh yes,' she gasped as each fresh salvo jetted straight into her womb. 'Oh yes, yes, yes!' She was sure she'd never been so heavily implanted. The mightiest flood since Noah took to his ark...

'Oh yes indeed!' grunted Slim, gritting his teeth and pumping his essence deep into her body with the greatest sense of euphoria he'd ever experienced in his life.

But at last he was spent, and with a sigh of regret he rolled off her beautiful bottom, giving it a farewell pat as he went. It had provided magnificent service. The most comfortable ride he could ever have wished for. In a flash his place was taken by Tim, almost before Slim's dripping wet tip had finally vacated her. Tim was on her back and inside her as Slim struggled to regain his feet, so fast that she wondered whether it was Tim, or whether Slim had suddenly discovered some hidden reserves. But Tim bit the back of her neck and she twisted and saw it was him. 'Ride her, cowboy!' he cried lustily, instantly following his own advice.

'Ohhh...' she gasped as he started to prod her with all his might. He was showing none of the subtleties earlier displayed by Slim, just carrying on from where the latter had so recently left off. Just ramming himself in and out of her already over-poked person as if his only ambition was to mingle his sperm with Slim's. Which, in truth, was entirely his concern. He'd waited so long that he wanted to shoot right away, as quickly as he was able. There'd be another chance later, he told himself as his fluid started to stir. In the meantime he'd settle for the fastest possible release of his excruciatingly pent-up frustrations...

Jennie could feel him reviving her climax - the very same one that Slim had been prompting such a short time earlier. The renewed thrusting was starting it up all over again. The deep delving and the streaks of fire across her buttocks were producing the same effect as before, so she laid stock still, savouring every moment.

Tim closed his eyes and concentrated on the sloshing sound he was creating inside her, far noisier than the earlier sound of Slim because now she was so much wetter. All Tim desired was to double the volume of seed she'd received so far, and Jennie groaned with pleasure as another heavy cargo of her favourite substance was suddenly discharged, jettisoned into her at a really blistering pace.

As a result of some rather hesitant encouragement, Jennie rolled over onto her back and blinked. 'Baby Jim,' she smiled happily as he kissed the side of her neck.

Very tenderly he ran a finger down the side of her face. 'You're really beautiful,' he breathed. 'The most beautiful lady in the world.'

'Thank you, Jim,' she whispered back. 'It isn't true, but it's very kind of you to say it.'

'I'm sorry about all this,' he whispered unsurely. 'It wasn't my idea.'

'Do you want your turn or not?' Slim snapped from the far side of the bed. 'If so you'd better get on with it.'

'Personally I think he's too young,' drawled Tim. 'Why don't we just cancel his go?'

Jennie wasted no time. She reached out and guided him down to her; concerned that Tim might actually implement his threat, and as he moved clumsily on top of her he kissed her on the lips. Only the second kiss of the afternoon. She'd been pawed and poked and pounded, but this was only the second kiss. She felt him begin to relax. She felt their bodies starting to melt into each other. She felt the instant rapport that seemed to exist between them.

'I love you, Jennie,' he murmured again, so quietly that only she heard it, and felt a warm glow inside. But this time it had nothing to do with any penis or implement. It was just a warm glow of pleasure at having been treated so nicely. And, she had to admit, at having someone on top of her whom she fancied quite a bit. How lovely to be shown some gentleness and consideration, she sighed to herself, as Jim kissed her tenderly. What a refreshing change. And how nice to be able to feel something that was a little bit like love and affection, as opposed to raw, naked lust. She could tell he was inexperienced, but that was also a welcome change.

Jennie reached down and cupped his throbbing erection. She really wanted him inside her. That was the difference between having Jim and having his friends. This time she really ached for him before he'd started, as opposed to when he was already embedded tightly inside her and making her come.

She used her hand to steer him in the right direction. She closed her eyes as he sank slowly and smoothly to the hilt. She could feel his iron-hard cock acting as a plunger and expelling much of the others' recently sewn seed. But Baby Jim would soon restock her, she sighed happily to herself.

'That's lovely,' she breathed, wrapping both arms around his neck and drawing his mouth back to hers, and they lay there, powerfully coupled but unmoving, taking turns to kiss each other and feeling the current flowing between them. Softly and sweetly she began to orgasm, relishing the taste of the kiss and the bulky presence of his penis as it pressed hard against the neck of her womb, still but very strong. At last she withdrew from the succulence of his mouth and smiled warmly into his face. 'Let's love each other some more,' she said softly, easing her hips upward as he slid his hands underneath the cheeks of her burning bottom and began to lick and nibble her magnificent breasts.

Epilogue

Now it's almost one hour later. Now all three young men have ejaculated. Ejaculated hotly and profusely. And Slim has also come on her face and in her mouth. Now Tim is lying on his back on the bed, securely inserted in Jennie as she lies on top of him. Slim is mounted on her back, buried hilt-deep in her bottom. Jim is sitting on the edge of the bed, near the headboard, watching his bloated erection sliding smoothly in and out of her lovely mouth. All three of them are intent on shooting into her as often as they can before the afternoon is done.

She's never felt so full, she thinks. She's nothing more than an overstuffed penis pie...

Slim starts to beat hard against the bounciness of her buttocks, making her wriggle and moan with delight. She can feel him so well in there. She can feel every contour of his elongated dick as it reams in and out of that ultra-tight passage. She's longing to feel him implant her in there.

'It's just as well there are three of us,' grunts Slim, picking up the pace even more. 'I suspect there's a great deal of fucking left in her yet.'

'But there won't be by the time we're finished,' mutters Tim, thrusting up with his groin and stretching her to capacity.

Jennie sighs to herself. She thinks he's probably right.

Chapter Two - The Tale of the Time Traveller's Wife

Michael Jamieson glanced down at the travelator on his left wrist as the galactic shuttle took the first jump through hyperspace. He was glad he'd made his decision. He was bored with life in the seventy-sixth century. In fact, he was bored with life in any of the centuries apart from the twentieth. For months he'd been wishing wholeheartedly that, two and a half years earlier, the beautiful raven-haired Sari had never stepped out of the future, fucked his brains out, and then taken him back with her to the amazing world of time travel. Was it too late to do something about it? No one really knew the answer to that, but he was determined to find out. Of course it was strictly illegal to return to your own time. Imperial law was very clear on that point. After all, what would be the consequences of meeting yourself? Or of changing some vital event in which you'd participated? And, if you did, exactly how prolonged and extensive would the chain reaction be?

No one knew the answer to these imponderables, so consequently you had to stay well away from your own lifetime once you'd vacated it for life in the future. If you didn't it was said that Imperial forces would come back for you - and that would be very bad news indeed...

But Michael wasn't concerned on that score. How would they know where you were? How would they know you weren't dozens of millennia in the future if you'd simply had your travelator programmed to tell lies? Just as he'd done two days earlier, when he'd decided to go back to the twenty-first century and make love to his gorgeous ex-wife for one last time. The black market programmer he'd found on Trident had charged him a fortune, of course. But he'd have no need for Imperial ecus once he was back in his own time. He intended to stay there, you see. He wasn't going back just to bounce the butt off his lovely Jennie - nice though that was going to be. He was intending to remain in his own era, albeit on the other side of Europe in order to minimise the risk of accidental self-confrontation. No one knew for sure the consequences of such a potentially disastrous mishap, although rumour had it that your two selves merged into one. But one what? If anyone had actually experienced it they'd never been known to tell the tale to another living soul.

It would take three days for the shuttle to return him to Earth. Earth in the seventy-sixth century. He had to get there before he could use his travelator, of course. Time travel is a marvel, but it's exactly what it says it is - travel through time. It doesn't enable you to travel through space as well. You have to do that in the boring old physical way. You have to buy a ticket for the shuttle and wait three whole days for it to transfer you across the galaxy, utilising the black holes that are to be found - so conveniently - in deep space.

Michael stood in what his travelator told him had, in 2000, been an open field close to his house. After all, he didn't want to travel back only to find he'd re-materialised inside a block of concrete! He set the co-ordinates so it would be the afternoon of Thursday, 6th July 2000. Jennie used to have every Thursday afternoon off work at that particular time of their lives together. That happy time before she'd begun to grow cool and distant toward him. That time, almost exactly one year before they'd divorced at her insistence. And as he stood there, adjusting his travelator, he still didn't understand why it had happened. Why she'd changed so drastically. He still had no idea at all how such a good marriage could possibly have unravelled itself over the course of just twelve months.

Six months after the divorce, Sari appeared out of nowhere and persuaded him to join her in her travels. That had been two and a half years earlier. Two and a half years before he'd stood there, in the seventy-sixth century, carefully setting the time controls. Two and a half years during which he'd roamed the centuries, finally losing touch with Sari somewhere in the fiftieth or fifty-first. Now he was returning to his own century - highly illegally - some eighteen months before he'd left it. He was returning to a point in his life some four years beforehand, to a time when their marriage was still joyful and still had twelve months to run.

Why did it have to be an afternoon for him to go back to visit his sexy young wife? Well, if it was an evening he would, in all probability, have walked into his house and found her there with another man. He'd have found her there with her husband (him). Her husband who, in 2000, worked in an office until five o'clock every weekday. So he had to travel back to see her at a time when he knew his other self would be safely out of the way. He had to set the travelator so he'd arrive at his house at about two o'clock - and thus have a clear three and a bit hours with her before his 2000 self returned home from work. He hoped she wouldn't notice he'd aged almost four years since he'd left the house that morning. He hoped he wouldn't return home unexpectedly from the office and surprise himself on the job!

The afternoon of 6th July 2000 was warm and sunny and he enjoyed the ten minute stroll to his house. The front door was locked and he'd long since lost his own keys, but the side door key was in its usual place under the flowerpot. Jennie's car was in the garage, so he knew she was home. He'd already decided to tell her he'd taken the afternoon off work, on impulse, so he could spend most of it plugged tightly inside her. She liked that sort of thing. She liked spur-of-the-moment surprises, particularly those of the carnal variety. It made her feel a bit special - which of course she was. And she was always keen on a spot of conjugal capers. Or rather, she was at that particular time of her life. It was only later that she started to change towards him.

He collected the key from its hiding place, and as he reached out for the deadlock he decided he'd also tell her he hadn't stopped daydreaming about her gorgeous bum all morning. Which was certainly true. In fact, come to think further, he'd been daydreaming about it all the way through the fifty-six centuries that followed that morning!

Because Jennie had the most perfect bottom that any husband could possibly desire - pert and pouting and honey-smooth to the touch. She had cheeks that bounced and swayed sexily from side to side as she walked. Cheeks so pretty and immaculate they gave him a sharp stab of real, physical pain whenever he glimpsed them naked or lightly knickered. And the rest of her was totally in keeping, from her blonde hair down to the high heels she always wore in order to emphasise her long, shapely legs.

They'd never tired of bedding each other. In fact, the sex had got steadily better and better as time sped happily by. Every morning and every night he'd make love to her - and some lunchtimes and afternoons, as well.

He walked in by the side door. The kitchen was empty, so he moved through to the lounge/diner. Abruptly he stopped and stared down at the floor in surprise. A pair of high heels and a short blue business skirt lay on the carpet at the foot of the stairs, a white silk blouse just beyond. He looked up. A frilly little half-cup bra was reposing on the second stair, and an even frillier pair of tiny white knickers dangled decoratively from the sixth stair from the bottom. The shoes, skirt, blouse, and undies were all too familiar. He looked up further and could see the legs of a pair of trousers hanging down from the landing. Passion had clearly overtaken the proprietor of those trousers in a very big way indeed. In the short distance from the foot to the top of the stairs the unknown man had stripped Jennie down to the buff and then exited his trousers at the first available opportunity. So this was how she used to spend her Thursday afternoons off work! But to his surprise his penis started to stiffen at the thought...

Stealthily he climbed the stairs. The landing was littered with the man's shoes, socks, shirt, tie, and underpants. The bedroom door was ajar, and there came ominous sounds from within. He peered through the gap on the hinged side, and although he was hidden from view most of the bedroom was visible to him.

Michael stood there, silent and still, his groin so rampant that he feared for the safety of his trouser fly. Jennie was curled up on the near side of the bed, wearing just a pair of silk stockings and frothy white suspenders. Her deliciously bare buttocks - framed so exquisitely by the suspenders and matching lace-topped stockings - were peeping up at him from less than six feet away, whilst her head moved steadily up and down over the groin of the hairy, naked man who lay at her side. In the wall mirror he had a clear view of the way she was fellating the long, thick, glistening-wet organ that was sliding smoothly in and out of her pretty mouth.

He stood transfixed to the spot, but amazingly felt no anger. Intense jealousy yes, but no overwhelming desire to break anyone's neck. It was simply one of the most exhilaratingly erotic experiences of his life. For some inexplicable reason he was absolutely fascinated by the spectacle of his own wife greedily sucking another man. He twisted his head to one side in an effort to identify the stranger. There was something vaguely familiar about him, but he couldn't quite say what. He felt sure he knew the man, but he just couldn't place him. Who the hell was this hairy-chested bastard lying on his very own bed and receiving a very proficient blowjob from his very own wife? He was beset with curiosity. How had the man made his way here? How had he insinuated his way into her favours? What right did he have to be enjoying himself so hugely...?

Then, at long last, the intruder sighed happily and turned towards him... and...

No, it wasn't his 2000 self at all. It was Jennie's boss from work. The pompous little prick who'd annoyed him so greatly during that cocktail party at the Royal Hotel. Well 'pompous' was a good description, but unfortunately the rest of that phrase most definitely was not.

How long had the affair subsisted? Was this the first time, or the hundred and first? Well at least now he knew why their marriage had simply fallen apart. Now he knew why she'd grown so cold towards him, and why divorce had followed no more than a year thereafter.

Michael stood there on the landing, his feet riveted to the carpet, watching Jennie perform with her mouth. Up and down she worked on her illicit lover, taking almost all of him inside despite his length and girth. Groaning with pleasure the man reached out and seized a more than generous handful of her gorgeous bottom, and then began squeezing and kneading it vigorously as she continued to suck. Michael stared intently at the white finger-marks produced by every far-from-gentle squeeze. He was consumed with a weird mixture of jealousy and desire. A form of masochistic pleasure, resulting from a wounded pride of possession, he supposed. The sight of the other man making free with her incredibly sexy rear was every bit as stimulating as watching her swallowing yard after yard of his seriously overgrown dick.

'I've spent the last three years longing to get my hands on you here,' growled the boss, using both hands to grip hard at the plumpest part of each pouting cheek and making her squawk with surprise.

For several minutes the giving of head continued, as did the ferocity of his hold on her bottom, but at last she lifted her head from his mid-section and gave him a sexy smile, one hand wrapped around his plum-coloured organ as it stretched and strained up towards his ribcage. Then she began to rub it back and forth across the side of her face. 'Don't stop sucking!' he gurgled painfully.

'Don't you want it down below?' she asked.

'Later. I want to come in your mouth first.'

'Don't use it all up, then,' she giggled, before returning him to the wet warmth of her mouth.

Michael could tell she was winning the battle. The man wouldn't be able to hold out against her much longer, he felt sure. He knew just how good she was. He knew how she could take a man right down her throat with ease. Suddenly the boss gasped and arched his back. 'Jesus!' he could only just manage to groan, before starting to spout like a fountain - all over her face and then into her open mouth. She couldn't keep up with him. His creamy-white fluid began to trickle thickly down one side of her chin; despite the way she was swallowing as fast as she could. 'Jesus!' he groaned again.

But at last he was spent. He lay back and stretched luxuriously while she continued to suck at the slowly shrinking penis she still held in her hand. After a while it wilted no further, remaining semi-erect in her mouth. Half hard and three-quarter size, it was, and then it started to stir. To stir and stiffen and swell. Quickly it regained its former stature, a proud pole of flesh ready to pillage and plunder once more. Ready to ravish Michael's lovely young wife in whatever way the man chose.

And ravish her he certainly did, rolling her onto her front and then mounting her prettily upturned bottom as if his life depended upon it. In and out of hot, wet pussy he thrust. In and out of the tight little passage that lay there waiting for him between sweetly dimpled cheeks. The tight little passage and sweetly dimpled cheeks she was supposed to keep only unto her husband! Smack! Smack! Smack! went groin against smooth bouncy buttocks as he tore happily in and out. Smack! Smack! Smack! Smack! Smack...! On and on and on, turning the cheeks of her bottom a most fetching shade of pink, just as if she'd been lightly spanked.

Michael gawped open-mouthed at the spectacle within. At the way those bouncing pink cheeks contrasted so nicely with the lacy white suspenders and stocking-tops by which they were surrounded on all four sides. It made him yearn to put her across his knee and colour them a great deal more. It made him yearn to transform the colour of that naughty little bottom from pale pink to glorious scarlet.

Faster and faster slapped rugged groin against pert buttocks, making her gasp and groan at the way she was being so comprehensively probed. Michael stood there, spellbound, watching the lover racing in and out between her succulent cheeks...

Now he was really dishing it out to her, pulling himself all the way out and then slamming his full length back inside as hard as he could. In addition to the smack of groin against bottom, Michael could also hear her vaginal juices squelching against the rigidity of each incoming thrust. Every time the man withdrew he could see, for a split second, her pretty pink lips wet and stretched and eagerly awaiting a return visit.

Now she just lay there, face-down in her suspenders and stockings, completely passive, groaning with pleasure as she let him have her howsoever he liked. Harder and harder he pumped, bouncing her up and down underneath him at an ever greater pace. Suddenly she began to orgasm violently, thrashing her head from side to side and wriggling her hips hard against him. Michael could see in the mirror the look of ecstasy on her face as her boss continued to fuck her at an impressive pace, as he continued to plunder pussy with a force Michael found hard to believe. It was the look he'd always assumed she reserved solely for him.

Another ten minutes or so slipped by, during which the fuck never slackened in speed. If anything it increased, and he had to admit a sort of grudging admiration for the job being done on her. He was only too well aware that he couldn't have done any better himself - if as well...

At long last the lover could hold back no longer and started to vent himself inside her, just as prodigiously as before, it seemed to Michael, making her squirm and squeal with delight. 'Oh, that's so good!' she groaned as he continued to empty himself deep within.

'You'll get some more in a while, I promise. You'll find I can do it three or four times in a row.'

'You're a sort of serial shagger?' she giggled back at him over her shoulder, through a mass of long blonde hair.

'It's easy with a girl like you.'

'How many girls have there been since you were married?'

'Lots,' he said with a shrug. 'What about you? How many men?'

'None, until now. Well, none except for last Christmas Eve at the office. But Christmas doesn't really count. Everyone does it, don't they? I expect Michael did too.'

'Why are you in bed with me, then?'

'I don't really know. I love Michael very much... I suppose I was just feeling extra randy for some reason...'

He slithered out of her with difficulty. 'Turn over,' he growled lasciviously. 'This time I want you from in front.'

'Good grief, you're still rock hard!' she squealed.

'I hope you're not complaining.'

'It's a bit too late for that now,' she murmured, sounding slightly rueful, her eyes glued to his rearing cock as she rolled onto her back.

'You're not starting to feel guilty, are you?'

'I suppose I am, a little.'

'Well, perhaps this will help take your mind off hubby...'

'Oh!' she squealed in startled surprise, full re-entry right up to the root having been accomplished in less time than it takes for an eye to twinkle, due to the highly receptive state of the opening in question.

Jennie closed her eyes. 'Oh gosh!' she moaned with pleasure, as penis proceeded to part pussy with consummate ease. 'You're starting me off all over again.'

Two minutes later Michael slipped away, an idea of breathtaking genius having suddenly occurred to him whilst watching his wife in the throes of ecstatic impalement.

The phone box was halfway down the road. Michael found the number quite quickly and was delighted to see that the boss lived just round the corner. The boss' wife answered almost at once.

'This is a well-wisher,' he began in an affected voice. Then he gave her his address. She recognised it immediately as the home of her husband's secretary. 'Your good husband is there,' Michael told her. 'Porking his rather-too-attractive secretary until she's purple. If you get round there now you'll see him leaving the house for yourself. In about five minutes' time, I should reckon. Goodbye.'

He waited until her car pulled up three doors down from his house. Then he phoned Jennie. She sounded a trifle breathless, almost as if she'd been disturbed in the middle of something energetic, he thought. 'Hello, darling,' he said brightly. 'I'm on the car phone. I've taken some time off work so we can go to

61

bed. I'll be with you in a couple of minutes or less. Bye-bye.'

He waited in the phone box with interest, and less than a minute later his front door burst open and out flew Jennie's boss, hurriedly buttoning his shirt, his jacket and tie in hand. His wife, an attractive brunette, stepped out of her car as he rushed by and swung her handbag viciously at his groin, felling him as if he'd been shot between the eyes, then she headed for the house clearly intent on tackling the 'other woman' while she was still *in flagrante delicto*. In other words, still freshly fucked.

As she vanished inside Michael made his way to the house too. The pompous little prick of a lover was lying on his side on the pavement, curled up in a ball. 'Help me!' he gurgled, desperately clutching his wounded parts in both hands.

'Certainly,' Michael said with a sympathetic smile, before planting the instep of his shoe in the centre of the man's arse with all the force he could muster. It felt so nice that he did it twice more. And then twice more after that. Then reluctantly he left the man where he lay in a heap and followed the wife's footsteps through the front door.

The lounge/diner was empty, but there were raised voices from above. 'Shagged him in your stockings and suspenders!' came the unmistakable scream of rage from the sorely wronged wife as he started to creep silently upstairs. 'You little bitch!' There was a thud, a crash, and a yelp of pain. The sounds of a brief skirmish followed, and then several loud slaps and much heightened shrieks of protest.

He peered through the bedroom door for the second time that afternoon, and for the second time that afternoon what a sight met his gaze! Jennie was now bent forward over the dressing table, her naked posterior pointing prettily up in the air. Bottles of perfume, cans of hairspray, hairbrushes, and various items of cosmetics littered the floor. The vengeful wife stood beside her, one hand brutally clutching a huge handful of Jennie's hair as it forced her head down onto the surface of the dressing table, her other clutching a plastic architect's ruler, XT3 variety, which Michael realised she must have snatched from his desk near the foot of the stairs. It was three feet in length and over a pound in weight. A very formidable instrument of chastisement indeed!

'Ouch!' howled Jennie as the ruler splattered noisily across the plumpest part of her bottom. He stared in wonder at the bouncing cheeks that were already starting to discolour before his eyes. 'Ouch!' she screeched as the ruler hit home once again.

'If I ever see you near him again, or near his office, you'll get far worse than this!'

'I won't, I prom—'

Slap!

'No, please don't—!'

Slap!

'No, not again—!'

Slap! Slap! Slap...!

Despite her struggles and screams Jennie's head was held firmly down while the ruler continued to rise and fall. The strength and determination of the infuriated older woman were simply too much for her to combat, so eventually she stopped resisting altogether and just passively accepted her punishment.

Slap! Slap! Slap!

'Yes,' panted the boss' wife, 'if you ever see him again, you little slut, you'll get far, far worse than this! Do you understand me?'

'Yes, of course I do!'

'Well just make sure you keep on understanding!'

The XT3 ruler rose above head height and then cracked down again. And again and again... and yet again after that. For the next several minutes Michael stood motionless, gazing in awe as one stinging blow after another landed loudly and painfully across soft buttocks that blazed with ever increasing intensity.

Michael found it an incredibly enthralling experience, watching the sweet little bottom that he knew and loved so well as it paid the penalty for its earlier misdemeanours. Watching as it paid in full for the way it had so grossly transgressed. What would he not have given to be wielding that heavy ruler himself! To have been the one punishing those unfaithful cheeks in the manner they so acutely deserved?

As for his wayward spouse, the shrieking had long since subsided, leaving her weeping profusely at the bitterness of her seemingly unending ordeal. 'I'm sorry,' she snuffled tearfully, her assailant having paused to regain her strength.

'You'll be even sorrier in a while,' came the unforgiving reply.

'But surely that's enough?'

'Not yet. Not by a long chalk. I'm just starting to enjoy myself.'

'Please let me go...'

'I told you, not yet.'

'You'll pull my hair out.'

'Keep still then. Stop trying to stand up.'

'Ohhh,' Jennie whimpered pitifully, tears spilling down her face once again as the chastisement was renewed with no less venom than before.

'Dirty little mare!' panted the other woman, laying the ruler across already blistered buttocks with all her might. 'I can even see the spunk running down your legs!'

'It'll never happen again!'

'It would have done if I hadn't found you out. Wouldn't it, you little whore?'

'I don't know—'

'Fucking my husband in your husband's own bed!'

'I said I'm sorry—'

'And I said you'll be a lot sorrier yet!'

'Please, you don't know how much it hurts.'

'Oh yes I do. I can tell from the colour of this randy little arse.' So saying, she laid the ruler to one side and sank her manicured fingernails deep into the offending object in question, provoking howls of anguished shock. For many long seconds she maintained her grip while Jennie wailed plaintively and writhed her hips from side to side in a forlorn attempt to break the hold.

'Scream as much as you like, little tart,' hissed the older woman, squeezing ferociously. 'It's no more than you've thoroughly earned.'

'Please let go!' howled Jennie, powerless to escape the torture being inflicted by the brightly painted nails. She tugged sharply sideways with her head, but that simply multiplied the discomfort she felt.

'Are you learning your lesson?'

'Yes!' she shrieked wildly. 'Oh *yes, yes, yes*.'

'You'll never fuck him again?'

'No, I swear I won't.'

'You'll never even set eyes on him again?'

'No, never, I promise faithfully. I swear I'll never set eyes on him again. I'll give up the job today. I don't want it any more.'

'Good.' The grip was gradually loosened and then finally broken completely, much to Jennie's obvious relief.

'Oh,' she groaned, wriggling with pain, 'you've scarred me for life.'

'I don't think so, you little tart. Much as you may have deserved it.'

The XT3 was retrieved from the top of the dressing table and swiftly put back to work. But despite the exigencies of the powerful ruler, the five deeply indented fingernail marks remained plain to see. Then the full force of the ruler was turned to the very tops of Jennie's exquisitely shapely thighs, instantly beginning to colour them as well.

Eventually Michael stole away, Jennie's tears still flowing and the fleshy crack, crack, crack of the spanking still raging unabated as he descended the stairs. It was time to take a leisurely stroll around the block, he decided. Even though he could easily have spent the rest of the day watching that delightful bottom being so mercilessly beaten alive.

When Michael returned to his house an hour later there was no sign of the boss' irate wife; just his own errant wife in the en-suite bathroom, rather more composed than when he'd last seen her. Jennie had evidently bathed and was wearing just a pair of little white knickers, similar to the ones he'd earlier seen discarded on the stairs. The rest of her clothes were folded neatly on a bedside chair, and he noticed there were already clean sheets on the bed. He smiled to himself at the way in which she made sure not to turn her back on him. What did she have to hide?

'I'm sorry I'm late,' he said. 'I bumped into Mark Walker in the garage and got talking.'

'That's okay. This is an unexpected surprise, anyway.'

She followed him through to the bedroom and he started to undress. 'I've been thinking about your little bum all morning and decided I couldn't wait until tonight, so I think I'll have a very generous slice of it right now.'

'Will you?' she giggled, blushing slightly as she lowered her bottom gracefully down on the bed, careful to keep her scantily pantied rear out of his view. But he'd already caught a glimpse of it in the wall mirror, the sweet little cheeks varying shades of crimson and scarlet where they peeped out from the tiny white covering stretched tightly across her. It would be fun to see how well she'd cope with trying to keep them out of sight, he decided.

'Lie on your front,' he suggested. 'I'd like to do it from behind.'

She blushed even more as she slid her undies daintily down her legs and off over her feet, before tossing them onto the floor. 'Couldn't I lie on top?' she said sweetly. 'That's how I fancy it. That way we can kiss as well.'

'I really do fancy mounting your bottom.'

'And I really fancy being on top. Can't we do it that way, Mikey? Please...?'

He relented, knowing her problem only too well and not wanting to tease too greatly. Seconds later she was astride him and he was buried deep inside her hot little chasm, experiencing the best erection he'd had for quite some time. The mental images of her romping in bed with her employer, and then being spanked by another woman, had lent incredible power to his loins. He wrapped his hands around her creamy-smooth buttocks, savouring the heat of their recent mistreatment, and proceeded to fuck her even better than she'd been fucked a short while earlier.

Eventually he started to swamp her, so profusely that he pictured her being swept off the bed with the tidal force of the emission. As he was voiding himself deep into her womb she bore hard against him and then began to climax again, as she so often did when she felt him boiling over inside her. He squeezed her buttocks hard in both hands, stoking up her orgasm, her mouth glued to his, her nipples brushing his chest and her hips writhing wildly with delight.

Stream after stream sluiced into her, and with each fresh eruption he thrust as hard as he could against her while she wriggled and squirmed and squealed, and gloried in the slavish acceptance of his seed...

'I'll just nip to the bathroom,' she breathed happily a couple of minutes later, staring into his eyes with an adoration he'd never quite seen before. 'Then I'll fix us a gin and tonic to share in bed.'

He chuckled to himself as she backed out of the room, studiously pointing her bare bottom away from him. But again she forgot about the mirror, thereby affording him the most exquisite portrait of soundly spanked cheeks snaking intriguingly from side to side while she reversed away from the bed.

As she closed the bathroom door he heard a car outside and then a key in the front door. But before he could react he was overcome with an unendurable fatigue. He simply couldn't keep his eyes open, try though he knew he must. After all, it had to be his 2000-self opening the door, he realised, but a second or so later he fell into a deep sleep, or trance...

Michael wasn't unconscious for long. Just a minute or two, at most. He came round as Jennie appeared back in the bedroom, a short, white bathrobe covering her nakedness, a glass of gin and tonic in one hand, and a wicked gleam in her eyes.

'That was a really lovely fuck,' she whispered, sitting gracefully on the edge of the bed. 'The best I've ever had.'

'Me too,' he replied truthfully.

'How could you come so much?'

He shrugged. 'I guess it's you.'

'And you were so big.'

'I know.'

Gingerly she wriggled her much sought-after tail end against the mattress, and winced. 'You hurt me, and I loved it.'

'I'm glad.'

'You made me come so much, too.'

'Yeah, I could tell.'

She took a sip from the glass. 'Let's finish this quickly and then do it again.' She uncrossed her legs and let the bathrobe fall open below the waist, allowing him to see how ready she was. 'You'd like that, wouldn't you?'

'Of course.' He took the drink from her and stood by the window to savour it. For no real reason he glanced down at his left wrist. His travelator was no longer there. A fairly expensive watch he'd purchased in 1995 had replaced it. It was just after half past five, exactly a couple of minutes after he would have returned home from work in his former lifetime.

He looked at his clothes. They were lying on the floor where he'd shed them. But they weren't his time travel garments. They were his 2000 gear. Quickly he turned to the wall mirror. The space-age hairstyle he'd assumed after Sari took him into the future was gone. His short black hair was definitely 2000-style. He looked back out of the window. His sleek black Saab turbo stood in the drive. It hadn't been there before.

'Is anything wrong?' asked Jennie, looking slightly concerned.

'I'm not sure,' he replied slowly. He picked up his trousers and sure enough his keys were in the pocket, together with his Visa card and cash. Again he peered in the mirror. He was definitely looking younger than he had of late. About four years younger, he reckoned. There was no denying the fact that he was his 2000 self again...

'Come back to bed,' urged his ravishing young wife, eyes sparkling like gems in the sunlight as she sat upright in bed, bathrobe now discarded and firm bare breasts on prominent display. 'Come back to bed and let's get in practice for that baby we're always talking about. I know twin boys run in your family, but I'm happy to take that risk. I'll stop taking the pill at the end of the month. Come back to bed and screw me as hard as you did before.'

So, Michael rather thought that he might...

He also rather thought that he now knew the answer; the answer to the question that plagues all those who travel in time. The question of what happens if you travel back to your own lifetime, quite illicitly, and come into contact with yourself. In his case, he decided, the answer was clear; you got the chance to sod-up the affair between your wife and her employer almost before it had started. You got the chance to sod it up and save your marriage and live happily ever after. At least, he sincerely hoped so.

But what of Sari? What if she turned up out of the future in eighteen months' time, just as she had before? Well, he knew one thing for sure; he wouldn't follow her back into the future. No way. He'd stay here in the twenty-first century with his wife. Assuming, of course, that the future divorce was now a thing of the past.

Just over an hour later Michael opened his eyes and gazed up at his bedroom ceiling. He'd been dreaming, and what an extraordinary dream it had been! Something about time travel and an erotic dark-haired girl he'd been bedding. He'd better not mention that latter part to Jennie. And he'd also dreamt something about Jennie's boss from work. That bumptious little dickhead who thought the sun went in when he pulled up his boxer shorts. Why on earth should he have been dreaming about that self-opinionated little turd? And what exactly had he been dreaming about him? For the life of him he couldn't remember...

He knew he'd taken the afternoon off work to spend it in bed with Jennie. They'd made love twice, incredibly passionately. That was still vividly in his mind. Then he must have fallen asleep and had some weird and wonderful dream. If only he could remember the details. What the hell had it been about? Something concerning a dark-haired girl, a divorce, and Jennie's boss at the office. And a spanking with a ruler. But he really couldn't recall anything more.

'I want to spend the next twenty-four hours in bed with you,' Jennie breathed hotly into his ear. 'Let's spend the next twenty-four hours shagging until we can't shag any more. You can do it, because you're your own boss. And I can do it too because I've packed in my job, with immediate effect. I don't think I can face working one more day for Mr Andrews. I'm going to concentrate on my beauty therapy instead. I've got all the qualifications now.'

Michael rolled on his side to face his wife. How strange. How strange that he should have some really peculiar dream about her employer, and now she'd just informed him that she was leaving work. What an odd coincidence.

Epilogue

Sari twiddled the dials on her video/tempo computer. Excellent! Everything had gone according to plan. The merger had been completely successful, and the end-of-chain reaction kept to manageable proportions. Just as she'd always assured the Temporal Star Council it would. And now, as a result, she could turn her attentions to the one hundred and forty-second century. She was aware that life there was even more lascivious, and there would now be this handsome hunk who'd also be in her guardianship, as well as desperately in need of help. He would be the three thousand and fourth male descendant of Michael and Jennie Jamieson. She couldn't wait to see how he compared in bed with his much earlier male forebear. God moves in mysterious ways, Her wonders to perform...!

Chapter Three - The Queen of Tarts

Tracie James, tall, slim, ravishing (and frequently ravished) stood on the pavement beside three of the regular hookers, her raven-black hair cropped short in a sort of urchin cut that perfectly suited her beautiful but decidedly mischievous face. The evening had not exactly panned out as she'd expected. Yes, there'd been sex all right, but not of the type she'd hoped would calm the desperate craving she still felt in her loins. The four fastest guns in the West had all got well and truly inside her, but they'd stayed for less time than it took to replace her undies after they'd done, leaving her even more unsatisfied than ever. Leaving her every bit as frustrated as she'd been before she'd hit on the idea of slaking her lust down here, on Whores Highway.

'Do all the men come so quickly?' Tracie asked the girl in red thigh-length boots and matching hotpants who stood to her right. 'It seems to be all over in just a couple of seconds.'

'Lots of them are like that,' said the girl. 'They're just after some instant relief, I guess. But sometimes you get a really good sorting out that brings you off, too. And quite often you'll get a few laughs as well.'

'Like Jillie and her husband's business colleague?'

'Yes. And Janet, for example. She's one of the very few who does it just for kicks. Anyway, a few weeks ago it was a very hot night and she was standing right here, wearing only her tiny knickers and bra, and showing off her sexy little bottom to every passing car. So this car drives up and out gets Sally, all freshly fucked and twenty pounds better off. The driver stares at Janet as she wriggles her hips in his direction, and she stares back over her shoulder at him. And guess what?'

'What?'

'The driver is her husband!'

'Oh my God!' gasped Tracie 'Whatever did they say to each other when they got home?'

'Lord knows. We haven't seen Janet any more since then.'

'I'm not surprised,' giggled Tracie.

'We haven't seen her husband either. I mean, he had some explaining to do as well. He'd just paid twenty pounds to shag Sally, after all.'

'Yes, but I bet he didn't look at it that way. I bet he was more concerned with the fact that his wife had been spending her evenings getting herself dicked by anyone who had the cash.'

'I think you're right,' sighed the other girl, stooping to peer into a passing car that didn't stop.

'Do you ever bump into any of your customers? At the bank, or in town, I mean.'

'Sometimes.'

'Isn't it embarrassing for you? Looking up from the counter, I mean, and having to deal with someone you were screwing the night before?'

'Very. But then again, it's usually even more embarrassing for the man concerned. Usually, but not always, unfortunately.'

'Tell me,' began Tracie, but she never got to finish her question. A bright red, open-topped Porsche pulled up at the pavement beside them. Tracie noticed at once that the female driver was an attractive, elegantly groomed girl about the same age as she was. The girl was expensively dressed in a light grey business suit and silk blouse. The skirt was short but extremely smart. There was something about her that Tracie instantly found exciting; the blonde hair, long legs and angel face. She was reminiscent of several girls she'd successfully bedded over the years, particularly Jennie Jamieson. So she felt certain she knew the type. A submissive, if ever there was one.

For several seconds the driver of the red Porsche stared uncertainly at Tracie. 'I don't suppose you go in for pussy?' she asked at last.

'I certainly do,' Tracie confirmed happily. 'It's one of my great specialities, in fact.'

The Porsche drove away, with Tracie in the passenger seat. 'I'm Rosalind,' said the girl. 'My husband, Jonathan, is away on business and I just fancied doing something a little bit different.'

'I know exactly what you mean,' laughed Tracie.

The car turned into an all but deserted car park and Tracie pointed to a spot on the far side. 'Park over there,' she suggested. 'It's nice and quiet, but there's enough light to see each other.

Rosalind stopped the car and turned to look Tracie in the face. 'I'd like you to make love to me,' she said simply. 'You can do anything you want.'

'Anything?'

'Yes, anything at all.'

Tracie decided to take her at her word. An opportunity such as this did not occur every day, unfortunately. 'You're a randy little trollop,' she said, before leaning over and kissing her hard with her tongue. 'I think I should start off by punishing you for having such an idea,' she continued when she'd finished the kiss. 'I think your fat little girlie bottom deserves to be taught a lesson it won't forget in a hurry.'

'Oh, I don't know about that.'

'You said I could do anything.'

'I didn't mean that.'

'And why not?'

'No one's ever done that to me before.'

'How old are you?'

'Twenty-seven.'

'Then it's high time someone did.'

'I don't see why.'

'Well, I do. If your husband won't give you what you need and deserve, then I'll just have to do it for him. It'll do you good.'

Rosalind looked nervous. 'Will you be nice to me afterwards?'

'Of course I will.'

'Do you think I should let you?'

'You might not be able to stop me. I can be very determined.'

'What am I supposed to do? If I agree, I mean?'

Tracie opened the passenger door and stepped out. 'We'll have to swap seats. I'll need you to be a little more accessible to me.'

Rosalind slid slowly and unsurely across to the passenger side of the car, allowing Tracie to gain the driver's seat. Tracie was delighted with the progress to date. This was going to improve the evening no end! She was already getting moist at the thought of the pleasure that lay ahead. 'So, you've never been spanked before?' she asked softly.

'No, never.'

'But you have had sex with a girl?'

'Yes. It's lovely.'

'But you don't like the idea of a soundly thrashed bottom?'

'No, not really.'

'Even if I told you it would double the pleasure to follow?'

'I really don't think so.'

Tracie decided it was time to finalise matters once and for all. It was going to be great fun to teach this sexy young lady the full, unmitigated truth about the gentle art of submission and the far from gentle art of domination. Particularly when the young lady concerned was sprawled, bare bottomed and totally subservient, across the polished leather seat of her hugely expensive sports car, undergoing the extremes of painful humiliation that Tracie fully intended to inflict. It would more than make up for the lack of sexual satisfaction so far that evening. 'Well, I'm going to do it to you anyway,' she declared. 'Whether you like it or not.'

'Oh...' Rosalind mumbled uncertainly.

Tracie leant across, placing a hand on Rosalind's silk-stockinged thighs just below the hem of her skirt. 'But first I'm going to be loving,' she said, sliding her hand underneath the skirt. 'So you'll know what you can look forward to once I've finished the punishment.'

Tracie's palm slipped past the stocking tops and glided over the smooth bare flesh beyond. 'Yes, that would be nice,' whispered Rosalind, parting her legs to allow the hand to explore further.

Once again Tracie kissed her, gently but hotly, and with a passion the other girl could easily detect. Her fingertips were now resting against the nicely filled crotch of tight silk knickers and she was savouring the satin-smooth texture of Rosalind's bare upper thighs, cool in contrast to the heat she could feel through the silk. Slowly she moved her fingers, stroking the lips she could feel inside. Immediately the knickers began to moisten 'Oooh...' sighed the female client, before Tracie kissed her again.

Back and forth worked the fingers, lightly and expertly, arousing the woman more and more with every second that passed. Now the crotch of the knickers was soaked, and Tracie could feel Rosalind's juices warm and slippery on her fingertips. She wasn't going to bring her off yet. She was going to give her a little more pleasure before it was time for the pain. Just as Peter had done to her so often in the past.

Rosalind moaned with desire as she felt one slim finger being pushed gently into her wet channel, all the way to the knuckle. Tracie left it there, unmoving, while she slid her tongue into the succulence of the other girl's mouth. At length she drew back and smiled sexily into Rosalind's face. 'You're very fuckable,' she whispered, starting to slide her finger slowly in and out. 'I wish I could do it to you.'

'I don't want to fuck. Not tonight. What you're doing is fine.'

The woman's juices were now seeping out of her. Tracie could feel them anointing her palm. 'Are you always this wet?' she asked.

'Not always.'

Tracie continued with the fingering, still very slowly and tenderly, making the girl wriggle her hips with pleasure. Then she used her thumb to touch the clitoris. 'Oh!' gasped Rosalind, surprised by the sudden shaft of pleasure that shot all the way up to her breasts. 'Oh, that's *good*.'

'Try not to come yet,' breathed Tracie. 'It'll be so much stronger and better if you can wait.'

'I'll try,' she croaked in reply, closing her eyes as Tracie kissed her once more, while the finger continued to pamper and please. This was the thing she always relished about being made love to by a girl, Rosalind reflected. The empathy and understanding of what was needed was so much greater than that of a man.

At last Tracie withdrew from the glorious wet warmth in which she'd been immersed, both above and below the suspender belt. 'Now I'm going to hurt you,' she said.

'How much?'

'A lot.'

'Will you love me again when you've finished?'

'Yes.'

'Do you promise?'

'Yes, I promise.'

'You'll be nice to me again?'

'Yes, Rosalind, I'll be so nice that you'll want to die. I know just what I'm doing.'

Rosalind was sure she did.

Tracie reclined the passenger seat as far as it would go. 'Kneel on the seat facing the back,' she commanded. 'And bend over it as far as you can. Get your head right down behind it. I want that ruttish little bottom stuck way up in the air.'

'You're sure you'll love me again later?'

'Yes, provided you do exactly as you're told.'

Reluctantly Rosalind obeyed.

'Pull your skirt up to your waist,' instructed Tracie, feeling her own juices flowing at the prospect of what was to come. 'And then your knickers down to your knees.' She switched on the interior light and gazed with approval at the pale, smoothly rounded cheeks bared for her. What a sexy little bottom it was! So delightfully plump and pert. It seemed to be pouting nervously up at her. And how pretty it looked in just those fancy suspenders. Slowly she ran a hand across both cheeks, savouring the firm, silky texture.

'So you're telling me that no one has spanked this lovely little bottom before?' she asked, kneading the flesh in her hand.

'That's right.'

'Not even your husband?'

'No.'

'Not even a girlfriend?'

'No.'

'If you were one of my girlfriends I'd put you across my knee regularly. Just to remind you what's what.'

'Thank heavens I'm not, then.'

Crack! Tracie's hand landed sharply on Rosalind's right cheek, making her squawk. 'Don't be impertinent!' she was warned.

'I'm sorry.'

'Haven't you ever wished that someone would do it to you?'

'I suppose I might have thought about it, once or twice. Wondered what it would be like, I mean.'

'Well, now you're going to find out.'

Very stealthily, so as not to give the game away, Tracie unbuckled and then unthreaded the heavy leather belt she was wearing round the top of her miniskirt. It was wide, with a square, solid brass buckle. Peter once used that buckle on her, she recalled, so she knew just how savagely it would bite.

Because the hood of the car was down there was ample room for Tracie to lift the belt above her head. 'Stay very still throughout,' she ordered, preparing to bring down the buckle end with all her force. 'Remember, you're to do exactly as I say. Shriek as much as you like, but don't move.'

'Aaaahhhhh!' Rosalind howled, the brass buckle having viciously seared itself deep into her right buttock, but she didn't dare struggle or try to shift position despite the excruciating pain.

Thwack! The buckle bit into her once again, with exactly the same response. And it did so again, leaving Tracie to stare in fascination at the suffering right cheek that now bore three raised prints of the buckle right across the fleshiest part.

'I thought you were going to use your hand,' sobbed Rosalind, tears rolling down her face as she wriggled her hips in despair.

'Do you want to have the best orgasm of your life when all this is done?'

'Yes, I suppose so.'

'Then stay as you are and accept it.'

Thwack! The evil brass buckle bit home for the fourth time on the same cheek, raising protests that were even louder than before. Tracie squeezed her thighs together and started a gentle climax that made her wriggle her own bottom from side to side. But she was wriggling with pleasure, not with the distress that was consuming the other girl.

But Rosalind still made no attempt to escape her fate, even though the belt rose and fell twice more on her right buttock, causing her face to contort in anguish. She'd never known pain like it. Her bottom was ablaze. She'd have to stay on her feet all through tomorrow's board meeting! Yet her insides felt even hotter. She could feel her vaginal oil seeping down both thighs...

Thwack! Thwack! Thwack! Now the buckle was burning her left cheek in the same way as it had the right. 'Poor little, sore little bottom,' tormented Tracie, bringing the belt down yet again. 'Poor little, sore little bum.'

The buckle had bitten into each cheek six times, so it was time for Tracie to return to the right cheek and start the process over, and when both cheeks had been dealt with again it was time to start on the right side for the third time.

'That's enough, please,' begged Rosalind. 'I can't take any more.' But she did. And then even more after that, until it was time for a hard spanking on top of the multitude of throbbing red welts, the change of tactics seeming to heighten the distress even further, much to Tracie's delight. 'Oh, no,' wailed Rosalind, weeping uncontrollably. 'Oh, that hurts so much. Please don't. I'm so sore already. Please, please can't you stop now? Surely that's enough?'

'A few more minutes,' insisted Tracie, smacking as hard as she could.

'Oh, that hurts.'

'It's meant to.'

'Oh! Ouch! Ow! Please, I just can't stand any more.'

'Well you're going to have to stand it.'

'I can't. I'm sorry, I'm sorry, but I just can't.'

'You can, Rosalind, and you will. Being sorry simply doesn't enter into it.'

'Oh don't, please, don't keep doing that.'

'Perhaps you'd prefer me to go back to the belt?'

'*No...*'

Tracie suddenly realised the extent of the suffering she'd inflicted. 'I'm sorry,' she whispered, slowly running her palm back and forth across the afflicted cheeks in an effort to soothe, and surprised to feel a teardrop trickling down the side of her face. 'Now I'll make it all up to you, just as I promised.'

Rosalind sat on the passenger seat, holding her breath and managing to stem the tears as she forced herself to ignore the pain and concentrate, instead, on the pleasures she hoped lay ahead. Tracie leant over and kissed her tenderly on the cheek, before reaching for the buttons of the girl's blouse. 'You've got a really pretty bottom,' she said with feeling. 'I'm sorry I've hurt it so much. I couldn't stop myself. It's so nice that I just had to keep on hurting it more and more.'

'I love you,' gulped Rosalind, wondering if she really was sitting on a bed of red-hot coals. How could anything as cold as that buckle burn so much? And how could such agonising pain make her insides knot with excitement so intensely?

'I love you too,' replied Tracie, her nimble fingers unbuttoning the front of Rosalind's blouse and then unfastening her bra. Her breasts were firm and full and creamy. 'You have beautiful nipples,' she sighed, taking them between finger and thumb.

'Thank you,' whispered Rosalind, snuggling happily back in the seat and allowing herself to savour the manner in which she was being so delicately explored. She loved the way she was now so open and available. She loved the feeling of vulnerability. This gorgeous raven-haired girl could do anything she liked to her... anything at all. She could hurt her again, or love her however she wanted.

Oh, those sweet, gentle hands on her breasts. How expertly she was being petted. And how wet she was between her thighs. This clever, clever girl was driving her to the brink...

Tracie lowered her hands and slid the already displaced panties over Rosalind's ankles and away. Then she parted the silk-stockinged thighs. 'And now I'm going to show you just how much I love you,' she purred. She lowered her head and began to lick, very delicately and deliberately, making the other girl groan with ecstasy. Slowly her tongue delved deeper and deeper.

'Oh, yesss...' moaned Rosalind.

At length Tracie lifted her head, her mouth and chin glistening. 'You taste delicious,' she breathed huskily. 'Here, let me share it with you.' She kissed her deeply once more, both girls relishing the salty-sweet flavour Tracie held on her lips.

Tracie's head was back between silky bare thighs, her lips and tongue hungrily devouring Rosalind, swallowing the plentiful juices until Rosalind felt herself wanting to swoon with the strength of passions aroused. She began to gyrate her hips, slowly to start with, pressing her groin into Tracie's face and then moving it up and down over her chin, lips and nose, much to Tracie's delight. Harder and faster worked Rosalind, gasping in disbelief at the pleasure she gained, both from the presence between her legs as well as the friction that further inflamed the cheeks of her wounded bottom. Harder and faster she worked, sobbing as she thrust against Tracie's wet face.

But then it was time to finish, and judging that her overwrought companion was as ready as ever she'd be, Tracie slid both hands between leather seat and hot buttocks and squeezed as viciously as she could. At the same time she lifted her head a fraction and sucked hard at the sweet little clitoris she now held in her lips. Rosalind screamed with the intensity of the climax provoked, while Tracie remained head down, sucking and squeezing as hard as she could.

'Can I drive this back?' asked Tracie, five minutes later, patting the steering wheel of the Porsche.

'Can you handle it, do you think?'

'Yeah, I'm a good driver. One of my ex-boyfriends had a Ferrari and I used to drive it quite a lot.'

'Okay then, take it for a spin down the motorway if you like.'

A few minutes later the needle on the speedometer was registering a hundred and twenty. Rosalind looked sideways at Tracie as the driver sat concentrating on the road ahead. 'So, you're married?' she asked at length.

'Yep.'

'Does your husband know you hang out on the street?'

'Not likely!' Tracie replied with a laugh.

'Why does a lovely girl like you have to do it? Do you really need the money so badly?'

Tracie smiled mischievously and shook her head. 'No, not at all. Tonight's my first time, actually. I just went down there because I was desperate for sex.'

'Just like me,' giggled Rosalind.

'I've had four men in an hour, and I'm still desperate. None of them lasted as long as a minute.'

The car roared down the slip road towards the next exit. 'I'm heading back there now,' said Tracie. 'Sooner or later I'll find someone who'll be able to give me a good shag.'

The Porsche was hurtling back along the southbound carriageway. 'Aren't you worried about speeding?' asked Rosalind.

Tracie shook her head again. 'Not at this time of night. Mind you, I did get caught once on a deserted road like this. In the Ferrari, doing well over a ton.'

'What happened? Did you get a ban?'

'No,' laughed Tracie. 'I bought the copper off.'

'How do you mean?'

'Well I could see he really fancied me as he stood there writing in his notebook. So what do you think I did?'

'You didn't fuck him, surely?'

'No, you're right, I didn't. Not quite.'

'What then?'

'I gave him a blowjob. With the driver's window wound right down he stood there on the hard shoulder while I sucked him off. I just reached out for his zip while he was telling me off, took out his cock, and gave him a quick blowjob. His colleague back in the car must have wondered what was going on, but I got the job done and was sent on my way with no more than a token slap on the wrist.'

They were now only five miles from town. 'You're really going back to the street?' Rosalind enquired, intrigued.

'Yes, until I get what I want.'

'I admire you,' Rosalind admitted. 'I'd never have the nerve to do that.'

'I've never been short of nerve,' Tracie said truthfully. 'That's the trouble, I suppose. If I was different I'd be too afraid of being caught out to fuck anyone I please.'

'You fuck anyone you fancy, even though your husband might find out?'

'That's just about it. But don't get the idea I don't respect him. I do, very much. It's just that my pussy rules my life, and unfortunately I have enough daring to let it. I just go out and get what I want. Sometimes I wish I was different.'

'He doesn't know what you get up to?'

'No. He frets and suspects, but he doesn't know. I wish I could be the wife he wants me to be. But we can't change who we are, can we?'

'No, I suppose we can't.'

'Provided Peter doesn't actually know, that's the best I can do. Keep him in the dark, I mean. I can't stop him being suspicious, can I? Hell, he'd still be suspicious even if I was the best behaved wife in the world.'

'Do you love him, Tracie?'

'I guess I probably do. Although I'm not totally certain what "love" means.'

'Who is?'

They were back to where they'd first met. 'I forgot to pay you,' said Rosalind, as Tracie reached for the door handle.

'Don't be silly. It was a labour of love.'

'But you must take something.'

'Not on your life,' Tracie declined again. 'I told you, I don't need the money.'

'Can we see each other again?'

'Possibly.'

Rosalind slipped a business card into Tracie's handbag. 'Phone me whenever you like. The sooner the better. Tomorrow?'

Tracie grinned mischievously. 'Don't you think you should give your bum a chance to recover first? I might decide to use a cane on it next.'

'Oh,' she gasped in surprise. 'Oh, you'll make me come just at the thought...'

Chapter Four - The Party's Over!

It was Saturday night and Tony was furious. It was scant consolation, but at least he perceived the chance to achieve something that, in three years of marriage to his attractive young wife, he'd always dreamed of achieving. He was furious because she'd absented herself from Alison's beach party for over half an hour. She'd absented herself with Peter James, one of her former work colleagues, and Tony was well aware of the fact that Kim fancied the socks off that particular so-and-so. Fancied him so much that she'd once told Tony she was 'lovesick' for him. 'Obsessed' with the thought of having him, she'd said. After the bombshell of that disclosure, two months earlier, following another party, she'd promised faithfully to avoid temptation and stay well away from him in the future. A promise she'd now broken so blatantly. Tony was consumed with jealous rage. Knowing how she felt about Peter he was certain they'd been up to no good. And that thought was agonisingly painful to him because he, in turn, fancied his wife as much as any man could.

'Just wait till I get you home!' he hissed angrily, staring at Kim's tightly trousered bottom as she settled it neatly onto the passenger seat of their car. 'I'm going to slap your fat little arse so hard you won't sit down for a week!'

'Why's that?' she asked after a pause.

'You bloody well know why. I warn you, don't make me any angrier than I already am.'

Kim thought it wise to take that advice, and said no more.

The rest of the journey was undertaken in total silence, apart from a few words with Tony's mother when their twelve-month-old son was collected from her house.

Kim carried the child into their lounge/diner, followed by Tony. She glanced apprehensively back at him and met his angry glare. 'Get the baby settled upstairs. Then take your trousers off and come back down here.'

She coloured, but decided it would be prudent not to argue. He glared balefully at the splendidly filled trouser-seat that slid impishly from side to side as she left the room, and experienced another sharp stab of physical pain. She was supposed to keep that unbelievably sexy little bottom for him, and him alone. God only knew the manner in which it had been behaving just a short while before...

He collected a high-backed chair from the dining area and placed it in the middle of the lounge, directly beneath the overhead light. Then he lit a cigarette and sank onto the settee, as livid as ever he'd been in his life.

Five minutes later Kim came downstairs, obediently wearing only the tight white sweater that finished at her navel, and a white cotton thong below. The black hipster trousers she'd worn earlier, and which Peter had much admired, were left upstairs exactly as ordered. Discretion, she'd told herself, was probably the greater part of valour... given the unfortunate circumstances. How had Tony noticed their absence when he'd been dancing so intimately with that sexy Jennie Jamieson, and there'd been about forty other people milling around in the semi-darkness? Oh dear, she should never have drunk that whole bottle of wine. She should know by now what she was like when she'd had too much to drink. She still blushed to the soles of her feet when she thought about what happened with Colin and Keith at the firm's Christmas party the year before last.

Kim saw the dining chair in the middle of the floor and coloured again, realising its significance. What should she do now? Stand still and wait to see what transpired?

'Bend over the back of the chair,' he instructed after a while. 'And stay bent over it until I'm ready.'

'Tony...' she began.

'Do as I say!' he snarled.

She dropped her eyes to the floor and moved hesitantly forward. She could see he was still absolutely seething, and she supposed he had every right.

'And don't bend your knees,' he added, lighting another cigarette.

Slowly she began to do as she'd been told, red-faced and embarrassed, and more than a trifle nervous as well. 'I said don't bend your knees,' he snapped, so she straightened them, standing as directed, head down, palms resting on the seat of the chair, tiny white thong pulled even more tightly than usual into the cleft between her cheeks: pale, exquisitely pert cheeks of which he'd always been jealously proud.

Tony stared at the saucily shaped bottom that had always fascinated him so greatly. In its present bent over pose it was even more alluring than usual, and the tight cotton thong concealed none of it from his wrathful gaze. The thought of what it might have been getting up to with Peter was anathema to him.

Mental images of exactly how it may have misbehaved itself flashed through his mind, torturing him further. So he decided to finish his cigarette before proceeding. The delay would give him time to absorb the situation...

At last he got to his feet and stood directly behind her. 'Oh!' she gasped in surprise, her thong having been suddenly and unceremoniously yanked down to her thighs. She'd rather hoped he'd spare her that indignity.

Once again Tony was unable to prevent himself visualising the way in which Peter had probably been making free with those saucy little cheeks just a short while earlier. And as he did so his anger grew even greater.

Kim screwed up her eyes and waited for what she knew was about to happen. But Tony just stood there, gazing angrily down at his wife's bare bottom. How far had it transgressed that evening? Had it ever transgressed all the way in the past? What had it been doing - and what had been done to it - at that office party two Christmases ago, when she'd come home very drunk and very late? How many times, if ever, since they'd married had it allowed itself to be bared for another man?

At length she felt constrained to speak. 'We didn't do anything terribly wrong,' she ventured.

'By which you mean you didn't actually let him fuck you?'

'That's right. I didn't.'

Kim always found it virtually impossible to tell a direct lie, so he tended to believe her. 'But you stood there in the woods at the back of the beach and let him do just about everything else?'

'I'm not going to say.'

'And you didn't let him fuck you, because by the time he got round to pressing the point you decided you'd already been gone too long?'

'I'm not going to say any more.'

'You would if you had nothing to hide.'

'I told you, I'm not going to say.'

Slap! Slap! Slap! Slap! Slap! Slap! Three on each cheek, with all his weight. She gasped and tears prickled her eyes, but she refused to shriek or protest.

'What did you get up to with him?' he demanded.

She said nothing.

Slap!

'Did you kiss him?'

'Yes.'

'And what else?'

'I'm not going to say.'

More hard slaps impacted, this time six on each buttock.

'What else?' She remained silent, so the treatment was repeated. 'Tell me what else you did,' he insisted.

More silence, so more of the same treatment, and then some more again. 'What else?' he repeated.

Another spell of silence, eventually interrupted by the prolonged sound of loud, hard smacks. 'I can keep this up all night if you want.'

'He unzipped my trousers...'

'And pulled them down?'

'Yes.'

Six more slaps on each side.

'And your thong?'

'Yes.'

The same treatment once more. 'Did you unzip his trousers?'

'Yes.'

'And hold his cock?'

'Yes.'

Six more stinging slaps on each cheek. Then the same again. 'And he stuck his fingers inside you?'

'I'm not going to—'

Slap! Slap! Slap! Slap! Slap! Slap! And then the same on the other side.

'And he stuck his fingers inside you?' Tony repeated heatedly.

Silence, so six and six more.

'Answer me!' But she didn't, so she suffered more of the same. 'Are you sure you really want this to last all night?'

'All right...' she panted, 'yes, he put his fingers inside me.'

'With his other hand all over this randy little arse?'

'Yes.'

'And you rubbing his dick?'

'Yes.'

Twelve times his hand landed on her left cheek, then twelve times on her right, but despite the intense discomfort she still refused to cry out or complain.

'How long did that last for?'

'I don't know.'

A good deal more slapping took place. 'Answer me!' he snarled when he stopped.

'About ten minutes, I suppose.'

'Did he make you come?'

'Yes.'

This time the slapping lasted even longer, so Kim clenched her teeth and bravely continued to try to blink back the tears.

'Did you make him come?'

'Yes.'

'In your mouth?'

'No.'

'In your hand?'

'Yes.'

'Did you swallow it afterwards?'

There was no reply, so the slapping resumed at pace.

'Did you swallow it?'

'Yes,' she finally admitted, and his response was exactly as she'd come to expect. She closed her eyes again and reminded herself that she had no option but to put up with it. She really couldn't blame him for being so cross.

The spanking stopped eventually. 'Did you promise to let him fuck you another time?'

It was the question she'd been dreading he'd ask. 'I'm not going to say.'

So he spanked her again until his arm was weary, while Kim stood there, her face contorted, but still suffering in silence. 'Will you answer me now?' he grunted at last. 'Did you arrange to let him fuck you some other time?'

'Yes.'

'When?'

'Monday. Instead of going to badminton with Jennie and Alison. Tracie's away on business, so I said I'd spend the evening with him. I'm sorry.' Kim closed her eyes and held her breath, waiting for the next fierce onslaught. But it never came.

'That's more like it. The whole truth at last. At least I assume there's nothing more to tell me?'

'Well, just one thing...'

'What's that?'

'I was going to let him have it tonight.'

'But?'

'But just as he was about to penetrate me he found he couldn't hold back any more. I suppose I'd been rubbing him a bit too hard, and a bit too long. Another second or so and he'd have come inside me, instead of in my hand. Although some of it did shoot over my tummy and pubes, and some between my thighs. I suppose I ought to tell you that I sucked the last few drops out of him, as well. After that he finished me off with his hand. I'm sorry...'

'Is there anything else I should know?'

'No, nothing.'

'You're sure?'

'Yes, positive.'

'So then, do you agree that you deserve what I've been doing to you?'

'Yes, Tony, I know I do.'

Tony slumped back onto the settee, deep in thought, and lit another cigarette, leaving Kim bent over the chair, red and raw to his view. Momentarily he reflected on the contrast in colour between the whiteness of her sweater and displaced thong and the poor, sore bum in between. At length he made up his mind. 'Would you like me to agree to you fucking him on Monday?' he asked, rather more gently than before.

'I don't think I ought to say.'

'Don't worry, I'm not going to spank you any more. So please answer truthfully, Kim.'

'I'm sure it would help.'

'Help you to get him out of your system, you mean?'

'Yes.'

'Do you really think so?'

'Yes, Tony, I do. Definitely.'

'If I agree, will you promise me two things?'

'What are they?'

'First, that you won't want to do it with him again?'

'Yes, I promise.'

'Can you be sure of that?'

'Yes, definitely, very sure.'

'And secondly, that you'll tell me about it afterwards. So there won't be any secrets between us.'

'Yes... that's a good idea. I'll tell you everything. In that way the only secret will be ours, because Peter won't know that you know.'

'That's true. I hadn't thought of it that way.'

She glanced back at him over her shoulder, vividly reddened buttocks pouting painfully in his direction as well. 'Don't you think you should punish me some more? I've certainly earned it. There's a bamboo cane in the shed you could use.'

He laughed, but not unkindly. Having reached his decision he was now coming to terms with the situation. 'I'd better not. After all, we need your pretty little bottom to be in mint condition for Peter on Monday evening. You wouldn't want it covered in lines and bruises when you give him his slice of it, would you?'

Her face blushed almost to the same shade as the grossly overheated object under debate. 'I suppose not,' she giggled uncertainly.

'But I could use it on you when you come home afterwards,' he mused, quickly warming to the idea.

Kim was suddenly less sure she should have mentioned the cane, but it was too late now to retract. 'I suppose that might help both of us feel better about what I've been up to,' she offered at length.

'Good. In that case I will. But right now you can stand up. I'm going to take you up to bed and fuck your brains out.'

'Mmm... that sounds nice...'

Epilogue

Two evenings later Kim was bent over the back of their leather settee, wearing nothing but a minuscule pair of semen-soaked knickers around the tops of her thighs, and a white T-shirt. Tony stood behind her, bamboo cane in hand, gazing down at the naughty bare bottom that had just spent the previous two and a bit hours romping in bed with Peter James. He was delighted that Kim had suggested this form of forgiveness for the way it had trespassed. Already he was feeling much happier about the way it had yielded itself up to Peter with such abandon. Kim, on the other hand, was having serious second thoughts as she waited for retribution to begin...

Tony tightened his grip on the long cane, pondering the details Kim had just finished confessing to him. Peter had found those beautifully sculpted cheeks an endless source of delight, she'd admitted. He'd been unable to keep his eyes and his hands off them all evening. So, as a result of the passion thus engendered, those bouncy pink cheeks found themselves misbehaving three times in a row! Three times in a row they offended! And throughout the third offence, which lasted for almost an hour, Peter had been mounted securely on top of them. For almost an hour she'd been spread facedown on the bed, a pillow tucked under her lower stomach and Peter kneeling above her, his knees straddling her thighs as he poked and probed with all his might. For almost an hour Peter was able to gaze down in awe at the sight of his groin slapping loudly and repeatedly into the fleshy-fullness of her buttocks, while his dick raced back and forth between them, impaling her all the way to the neck of her womb, again and again and again...

In fact, if he looked closely he could actually see the slight discoloration that the constant slapping of groin against bottom had produced. The very roundest part of each mouth-wateringly pert cheek was definitely a few shades pinker than the rest of her bottom. A visible testament to the way in which she'd been so thoroughly skewered and screwed, before finally being pumped full of yet more seed.

Kim sensed him lifting the cane on high, and turned her head to look back at him over her shoulder. 'I'm sorry,' she whispered nervously. 'It'll never happen again. It's all over with Peter. I love you just as much as I ever did.'

'And I love you just the same, too.'

'Owww!' she howled, Tony having raised the first of the many fiery lines he intended to paint across those unfaithful, but still much adored, cheeks.

Chapter Five - In the Arms of the Law

Sixty minutes after the arrests the scene at Westminster police station was as follows: Jennie Jamieson - aged twenty-six, and as drop-dead gorgeous as the polar day is long - stood in front of the desk, together with the rest of the girls from the massage parlour and six plain-clothed officers from North Westminster CID. The duty inspector sat behind the desk, taking an official note of the complaint.

'The raid commenced at five p.m.,' Detective Sergeant Sherman said to the inspector. 'Acting on information received.'

'Quite so,' murmured the inspector.

'All three massage rooms were visited simultaneously,' continued DS Sherman. 'Together with the showers beside the sauna.'

'Start with the showers.'

'The showers were inspected by DC Simpson. Two naked people were discovered in one of them, a man and the defendant Lucas, who admitted she was in charge of the premises. The defendant Lucas was kneeling on the floor, performing a sexual act with the man.'

'Which was?' asked the inspector.

'According to DC Simpson, the man's penis was in her mouth.

'DC Green and I visited massage room number one. The defendant Jamieson was lying face down on the bed, wearing only stockings and suspenders. A naked male client was lying on her back. The defendant was squealing whilst the man's groin was moving up and down on top of her buttocks. They were engaged in sexual union.'

'How do you know that, sergeant?'

'We had to wait in the room until they finished. There were only two officers present, and I felt it would have been injudicious to try to interfere with the male customer, bearing in mind his size and the fact he'd threatened to 'waste' us if we tried to stop him. This was despite the fact that we'd already shown him our warrant cards and informed him that the young lady with whom he was fornicating was under arrest.'

'I see. For how long, then, did the two of you observe the defendant Jamieson in the act of sexual congress with this man?'

'Three or four minutes at least, sir. So we were left in no doubt as to what the couple were doing.'

'Did she say anything when the man had finally finished?'

'Yes, sir, she asked permission to visit the toilet.'

'Which was granted?'

'Yes, inspector. We felt that in the circumstances we ought to agree.'

'Yes, quite. I've no complaint about the way you conducted yourselves in that respect.'

'The defendant was then allowed to dress in her ordinary clothes.'

'Her ordinary clothes?'

'As opposed to the uniform the girls wear at the parlour when they're working, inspector.'

'Oh, I see.'

The detective sergeant dropped his gaze to the lovely long legs that stretched down from below the hem of Jennie's short skirt. 'Although I believe she retained the white silk stockings and suspenders,' he continued. 'In her haste to get dressed, I mean. And also the undergarment that goes with them.'

'The undergarment?'

'The matching satin knickers, inspector.'

'You're not suggesting a case of theft?' asked the inspector, also staring intently at the lower half of Jennie's person for rather longer than seemed necessary.

'Oh, no sir, not at all. Just a charge of conspiracy to run a disorderly house.'

'Very well, take her to an interview room with Detective Constable Greene and a WPC.'

DS Sherman turned to Jennie. 'You're not obliged to say anything unless you wish to do so,' he cautioned her. 'But anything you do say will be taken down in writing and may be used in evidence at your trial.'

'I feel a bit faint,' she whispered.

Fifteen minutes later Jennie signed her written confession of guilt. 'Oh good grief,' she groaned in despair. 'What on earth am I going to say to my husband?'

'Doesn't he know you're on the game?' the sergeant asked, not unkindly.

'I'm not on the game,' she snapped indignantly. 'I'm a respectably married woman.'

The sergeant picked the signed statement up from the table. 'You say in here that during the course of today you've had full sexual intercourse with three different men, and performed other acts of oral sex and masturbation. In return, you've been paid a total of four hundred pounds. If that's not common prostitution then I'd like to know what is.'

Jennie stared down at the carpet. 'But I've never done it before,' she whispered at length. 'Sex for money, I mean. I was just helping out because they were short-staffed. Short of professional masseurs, I mean. I didn't know I'd be expected to offer the *extras* as well. I've never worked in a massage parlour before, you see. Only a proper beauty salon. I was just expecting to massage a few customers for twenty pounds a time. I realise I should have refused to do the sex things, but it wasn't just because of the money. I was feeling, sort of, horny... and the men were really nice. I didn't think there'd be any harm in it.'

'I understand what you're saying,' said the rather pretty young woman police constable who was sitting in the corner of the interview room, notebook and pen in hand. 'But what you've done is against the law.'

'Do you really have to charge me?' pleaded Jennie. 'Couldn't you just caution me instead?'

'We could,' replied Detective Constable Greene, the third police officer present. 'But this is far too flagrant a breach for simply a caution. This is a case of a full-scale brothel operating blatantly right in the very centre of London. It will have to go to court, I'm afraid.'

'But my husband,' she whispered, teardrops showing in her eyes. 'What about Michael? Whatever is he going to think? Whatever are other people going to think? What about my parents, and my young children? Surely you could stretch a point and caution me instead? Please, couldn't you do that for me?'

'We could,' the detective sergeant said slowly, 'but the point is whether we should.'

'I'll never do it again. I'll never do it for money again. I've definitely learnt my lesson.'

The two men looked at each other thoughtfully. Then the uniformed WPC plucked up sufficient courage to suggest something that had just occurred to her. 'Suppose she was cautioned in conjunction with some other punishment...' she said carefully, feeling the crotch of her knickers dampen at the thought of what she was about to propose. 'Some form of corporal punishment, for instance...'

There followed a weighty silence, during which all four of them pondered the various implications of the suggestion - the police officers with considerable intrigue, Jennie with mixed emotions. She'd been down that road before. Indeed, she was, of course, to go down it more then once again, but at that particular moment she was blissfully unaware of her future appointment with Mr Stanley's long, leather-bound cane.

The men looked at each other again. 'I suppose that's a possibility,' Detective Sergeant Sherman replied at length, his chin cupped pensively in one hand.

'I think it is,' mused the detective constable, who sat at the same side of the table. 'I think it probably is...'

'It is her first offence,' urged the attractive WPC, wriggling her hips ever so slightly. 'I do think she deserves a helping hand.' She coloured at the realisation that her words had been more appropriate than she'd intended.

'The manager, Mrs Lucas, did confirm that Jennie is a fully qualified beauty therapist,' the DC pointed out. 'And that this was the first time she'd ever worked at the parlour. That corroborates part of what she's just told us.'

The sergeant turned to the policewoman. 'You're sure there are no previous convictions?'

'Yes, sergeant, the computer's completely clear. There are no possible ambiguities.'

'We could just about persuade the inspector that a caution had been the appropriate action to take,' murmured the detective constable. 'He might not be ecstatic at what we've done, but it's just about justifiable.'

'Jennie's a married woman,' said the WPC. 'We could point out to the inspector that the disastrous effect of a conviction on her marriage would have been disproportionate to the facts of the offence itself.'

'She also has a young family to consider,' added DC Greene. 'Two-year-old twin boys. Surely the inspector would expect us to take that into account as well?'

'What are your views on the matter?' the detective sergeant asked Jennie, after a further pause for thought. 'We couldn't proceed in that manner except with your approval.'

Jennie took a deep breath. 'It would be better than having to go to court...'

Jennie was told to stand up and remove her miniskirt. This she did, blushing demurely as it fell to the floor by her feet. For several long seconds all three officers stared appreciatively at the tiny white knickers, so perfectly filled, and the matching suspenders and stockings. Then she was ordered to bend over the knee of the lady constable, who was still sitting in the corner of the room. 'That's right,' said the woman police officer as Jennie settled herself as comfortably as she could across her lap, hands and toes resting on the floor.

No one present could prevent themselves feasting their eyes on those spectacular, upthrust buttocks, garnished so sparsely in tightly stretched satin; the merest scrap of flimsy white satin now stretched to the limit of its endurance across the pouting pink cheeks of her bottom. Jennie knew only too well that the tiny little garment only served as decoration. That it only served to emphasise how exposed and vulnerable she was in that juicy-ripe part of her person upon which the upholders of the law clearly intended to exact retribution.

The lady PC gazed down in delight at the skimpily knickered bottom draped submissively across her knee. It really was perfection itself! Nothing could have been done to improve it by one iota. Absolutely nothing at all. Except, of course, to transform it from pale, creamy-smooth pink to a much, much darker hue. Which she fully intended to do...

The WPC laid her hand across the centre of Jennie's right cheek, relishing the warmth and springiness she could feel beneath her fingers and palm. Relishing, also, the way in which the bare flesh seemed to possess almost the same slippery-smooth texture as the seat of the satin knickers. This was the area to which she would direct the first assault. Jennie closed her eyes and waited for what she knew to expect next.

'Spank her, WPC Gilmore,' the sergeant growled at last, swallowing hard as he spoke. 'Through her knickers to start with, and then on her bare buttocks as hard as you please.'

Ten minutes later the satin knickers were around Jennie's knees and her bottom was starting to glow as brightly as a beacon at night. But still the WPC's hand continued to crack down on one reddened cheek after the other. Noisily and remorselessly it impacted, improving the colour with every slap. On and on she smacked, and the redder Jennie became the faster she struck. It was lucky the interview room was soundproofed, Jennie thought, tears rolling down her face. Otherwise they'd be able to hear her ordeal all over the police station. And how embarrassing that would be! How embarrassing, having to walk out of the place knowing everyone was aware of the fact that she'd just been soundly spanked!

The two male officers stared in fascination as one loud, ringing smack after another landed on target. What a privilege it was! Not only was this the prettiest bottom they'd ever seen, but now it was the reddest as well - and gaining colour by the moment. First they'd watched it being mounted by the huge American back at the massage parlour, and now they were being treated to the sight of it being set ablaze by the sexy little WPC, who now adjusted Jennie's position and began to slap hard across the centre of both cheeks at the same time, turning the high points an even brighter shade of red.

The WPC was really warming to her task. She was laying into Jennie with a strength that belied her slim build. On and on she spanked, relishing every smack and every tearful sob and squeal. The excitement was so great that her knickers were already soaked through. This was the most fun she'd ever had, she thought as she slapped and slapped and slapped. This was truly wondrous; punishing this delicious bare bottom in the manner it so richly deserved. She just loved the way it bounced and reddened with every stinging rebuke. And the more fiercely she punished it, the hornier she felt...

For years she'd secretly fantasised about spanking another girl, particularly a beautiful blonde with a really cheeky, inviting arse, such as this one.

If only she had a whip, the WPC sighed to herself, squeezing her thighs together and then gasping softly at the sudden pang of pleasure that shot through her loins. Or a long cane, she thought, pressing her legs together even more firmly, and gasping again at the mental image of Jennie's beautiful bottom brutally striped with six raised welts. But for the time being she'd have to make do with the use of her hand.

The WPC gritted her teeth and continued to slap with all her might. Half a dozen times on one side, then half a dozen on the other, wanting to punish those naked cheeks just as thoroughly as she could. How splendidly they now contrasted in colour with the snowy white suspenders and stocking tops.

'Ohhh...' Jennie sobbed, staring down at the tearstained patch of carpet just below her face. She wriggled her hips from side to side in discomfort as the tears continued to drip. How humiliating, having to lie like this in front of the men while the lady PC spanked her poor, poor bottom. Spanked it with such energy and enthusiasm that it was obvious she was thoroughly enjoying herself. But where on earth was the enjoyment? Where was the enjoyment for a girl in spanking another girl's bottom? For the life of her she couldn't see it, but on the other hand she was aware that a lot of girls could. She knew it from previous experience. She knew it from the way Tracie James, and also her cousin Jean, had dealt with her in the past.

But, painful and humiliating as it was, it was still far preferable to the alternative - having to face criminal charges in front of a court of law.

The male officers sat still, watching intently as the WPC's hand proceeded at a blistering pace. She was perspiring from her exertions, but the punishment didn't slacken at all. Eventually, however, she did pause in order to admire her handiwork. With great satisfaction she gazed down at the hot cheeks that lay submissively over her lap, savouring not only the sight of freshly spanked buttocks, but also the sound of muted sobbing.

But the sheer impudence of that lovely bottom suddenly infuriated her further, so once again she began to slap the fattest part of each bouncing cheek, applying all the strength she could muster to the shapely bottom framed so exquisitely with frothy white lace as it reddened and quivered. Of clemency there was none; the police officer's only concern was to inflict as much suffering as she could on the bright red globes she had at her mercy.

Jennie kept her eyes tightly shut, weeping in silence because she no longer had the energy to squeal or gasp. She must try to concentrate on something else, she told herself. But the only thing she could think about was the time after the ladies football match when the captain, Tracie James, put her over her knee on that bench outside the changing room and spent a good ten minutes using a shin-pad on her bare bottom - for having missed the vital penalty that cost the team the cup. Right in front of the other players, Tracie had done it. The players from both sides, that is. As well as the male referee and linesmen! How embarrassing it had been at the party afterwards, with everyone - particularly the men - making all sorts of saucy remarks about her blistered bottom. Although the upside had been halfway through the party, when Tracie insisted on taking her outside and giving her a really lovely pussy-petting, by way of compensation ..

Oh God, she was well and truly alight! Every slap seemed to sting more than the one before. She'd never be able to sit down for a week! Her bottom felt as if the WPC had poured petrol all over it, and then set fire to it with a match. And it was becoming hotter and more tender by the second. No one had ever spanked her so soundly before. Not even Michael after he'd found out about Jonathan Ward and that beach hut. How much longer was this going to continue?

Had the WPC been able to hear the question she would have replied, 'Until I'm too tired to lift my hand above my head.' But Jennie was able to gauge that much for herself. Her tormentor was showing not the slightest sign of relenting. Tight-lipped and even more determined than ever, she was now delivering a dozen of the best on one cheek, a dozen of the best on the other, and then another dozen of the same across the centre of both, savouring the effect she was creating across those brightly burning high points. She groaned to herself with pleasure. There was nothing as exhilarating as treating such a gorgeous bottom this way! It was just so unbelievably inviting; the most spankable bottom imaginable. Oh, what wouldn't she give to be wielding a cane!

But wait. There were those stout wooden coat hangers in the cupboard beside the door. The ones that were used by the uniformed branch for their heavy-duty overcoats...

'Stand up and bend over the table in the corner,' ordered the WPC.

'Why's that?' sobbed Jennie, starting to edge herself back in order to get to her feet.

'For the next part of your punishment.'

Jennie rested her torso flat on the tabletop, gripping the edges tightly with both hands as she waited in apprehension. What was happening now?

'Owww!' she yelped, jerking back her head in surprise at the sudden switch from hand to unyielding wood. 'Owww!' she yelped again.

'I think that's enough,' the detective sergeant said at long last, much to Jennie's relief. 'I think you've made your point felt.'

'Are you sure?' panted the woman police constable, very reluctant to stop. 'I was just getting into the swing of things. I was about to ask if I could borrow your belt.'

The sergeant moved behind her and placed his hands on her shoulders. 'My trousers might fall down if you did that,' he murmured into her ear.

'Perhaps that wouldn't be such a bad idea,' she breathed thickly, pushing her buttocks back against him.

'It can soon be arranged.'

She wriggled her neatly uniformed hips. 'What a strange place to keep your truncheon...'

'I'd better free it, then.'

She turned to face him. 'Here, let me help.'

Detective Constable Greene was now standing directly behind the exhausted form of Jennie. 'We've got a head start on them,' he muttered, staring down at her naked bottom. 'If you stay exactly as you are we could be the first to get underway. What do you say?'

Jennie glanced wearily at him over her shoulder, feeling a sharp pang of delicious anticipation. The vivid reddening of her bottom had worked a truly inexplicable spell on her, as well as on the others. All four of them were as hot and randy as ever they'd been. 'Okay,' she whispered, colouring prettily.

Both girls were being vigorously fucked from behind. Both of them were bent forward over the table, side by side, Jennie's white stockings and fiery red bottom contrasting nicely with the WPC's regulation dark blue stockings and pale, creamy-white cheeks. Side by side, also, stood the two male officers, each enjoying the spectacle of the bottom he was mounting, as well as the one beside. Slap, slap, slap went hairy groin against bouncy buttocks, as the men piled into the girls with glee.

After a while the men swapped over, each sinking into his new partner with verve and enthusiasm. Then the chase was on as before, as if the men were in competition with each other.

On and on they raced, eagerly pumping themselves lustily into their partners, eagerly forging in and out with gusto. Then the partners were swapped again, and eventually the woman police constable was mightily implanted by the detective sergeant, gasping as she felt his seed coating her womb. By the time the constable ejaculated into Jennie the sergeant was up and ready for more, so he took over on Jennie while his junior quickly recovered and then fucked the WPC, until once again they came and the girls now bore a stickily mixed load.

Ten minutes later, the men had recovered yet again and both girls were stripped down to their stockings and suspenders. Jennie lay on her back on the table, her thighs wrapped round the sergeant's waist. As he moved smoothly in and out the WPC was leaning over her, kissing her sweetly and fondling her beautiful breasts. To complete the tableau the detective constable was once more behind the policewoman, his hands gripping her tightly round the waist while he impaled her with long, steady strokes of considerable weight and power.

Jennie sighed with pleasure. It was like being made love to three times over. Not only did she have DS Sherman working away inside her, but as she and the WPC kissed she could almost feel the constable's penis working away in the other girl. Indeed, it was almost as if he was inside her as well as the WPC.

The lovemaking proceeded slowly and smoothly, and with her mouth invaded by the WPC's succulent little tongue, Jennie felt the sergeant slip his hands under her buttocks and push a fingertip into her bottom. The effect was electric and her orgasm was instantly revived. Sensing the girl would wish to experience the same thrill, Jennie reached for her, and immediately the WPC started to spasm as well. Tears of pleasure meandered and mingled on their cheeks as they hugged and kissed each other, and wriggled their hips in delight.

The WPC lifted her face for a moment, her eyes bright and staring. 'I love you,' she groaned with feeling.

'I love you, too,' Jennie replied.

Then they were kissing again, even more fervently than before, hands delicately cupping breasts and bottoms as they squirmed and sighed with pleasure.

Inflamed by the sight of the lesbian love the men gritted their teeth and fucked as fast as they could, but eventually, inevitably, they were exhausted and spent. They flopped down onto chairs, leaving the girls still locked in each other's arms on the table, lips together, hands and fingers exploring. Softly and gently they started to climax, sighing sweetly as they did so. For several long minutes they shared it, the men staring in fascination as the girls squirmed tenderly in each other's loving embrace, each instinctively knowing the needs of the other.

But finally it was over. With a sigh of regret they separated and stood again on unsteady feet, both of them flushed and short of breath. 'That was lovely,' sighed the WPC, looking round for her clothes. 'I'm sorry about your bottom. I got carried away completely.'

'I think I'm starting to get used to it,' said Jennie, stooping as demurely as possible to collect her scattered garments from the floor. 'There seems to be something about my posterior that attracts major abuse.'

'There certainly is,' the detective sergeant agreed with feeling, his eyes glued to the blazing object in question, as were the eyes of the other two officers present.

'Can I go now?' Jennie asked over her shoulder, the cheeks of her pouting bare bottom wriggling provocatively from side to side as she fastened her bra. 'When I'm dressed, I mean,' she added, by way of clarification.

Chapter Six - Sexopoly

Jan stared in dismay as the dice rolled across the dining table and finally came to a stop. Two sixes! The game of Sexopoly was over and she'd just lost. She was to be the victim. Of course, she'd always realised it might end this way. But she'd rather hoped - indeed, expected - that it would be one of the seven other people present who'd end up in this situation. She'd rather hoped it would be either Tommy, her husband, or someone from the other three young couples who'd have to pay the price of defeat. What would be demanded of her by way of a forfeit? What would she be expected to do in front of her husband and friends?

It seemed like a bit of a giggle at the start - agreeing to play a sex game. But the minor forfeits they'd all had to pay during the course of the board game had shown that the penalties for failure might be rather higher than she'd originally assumed. The kissing and touching for instance, albeit fairly innocent thus far. And the way the dice had obliged Jennie Jamieson to spend ten minutes upstairs with Jonathan, doing to each other whatever they agreed. Actually, knowing Jennie, the mind boggled as to what the two of them might have got up to together. Certainly she hadn't liked to look Michael in the eye when she came back down, more than a trifle flushed in the face. Mind you, if the dice had forced her to leave the room with Jonathan, she didn't like to think about what she might have been prepared to let him do to her. Nor whether she'd have been able to look at Tommy on her return, innocent or not...

Well, it wasn't really her fault if she fancied that good-for-nothing womaniser, Jonathan Crowe. She couldn't help how she felt. She couldn't stop herself wanting to have him, try as she might. Did Tommy guess how it was? She'd done her best to hide her feelings from him. It was so wrong, after all. Jonathan was his oldest and closest friend, so there was no way she was supposed to hanker after his dick.

Rosalind interrupted Jan's thoughts. Rosalind was the Games Master, and therefore in charge of proceedings. It was her dinner party - well, hers and Jonathan's, to be precise. So she'd been elected to be in charge of the board game that Alison and her own Michael had brought along for after the meal.

'Roll the dice,' Rosalind said to Jan. 'Just one this time.'

'What for?'

'To determine the level.'

'To determine the level of what?'

'The level of forfeit, of course.'

'Oh, I see.'

'Go on, then. Roll one dice and then we'll be able to find out what happens next.'

'Don't throw another six,' Michael warned her cheerfully. 'That's the highest level. The severest level of forfeit there is.'

Jan threw the dice. Four! It could have been better, she mused, but at least she wouldn't be playing at levels five or six. What would level four entail? Nothing too horrendous, surely...

Rosalind broke open a sealed envelope marked *Forfeit - Female Player - Level Four* and began to read the printed card inside. 'First you have to choose a male partner,' she explained. 'You have to choose left or right.'

Jan sighed with relief. Jonathan was sitting to her left, while her husband, Tommy, was on her right. 'Right,' she said at once, giving Tommy a quick smile. That would reassure him; that would make him feel good about things; about any simmering suspicions he might have as to her feelings for Jonathan.

'Okay,' said Rosalind, 'according to these instructions your male partner is the one on whose right you are sitting.'

'Oh,' Jan squealed in annoyance. 'That's not fair at all.'

'But it's what it says here, I'm afraid. If you'd said *left*, then Tommy would be your partner.'

'It's very misleading.'

'Nevertheless, it's how the game's to be played.'

'Suppose Jonathan refuses to be my partner?' she asked hopefully.

'He can't,' Rosalind replied firmly.

'And in any event, he won't,' Jonathan confirmed with a grin. 'I'm looking forward to it.'

'I bet you are,' said Rosalind, his wife, frowning.

'What does she have to do?' enquired Tommy, trying to sound unconcerned. He stared down at the luridly illustrated game board spread out on the table in front of him. The game itself was very similar to *Snakes and Ladders*, except you travelled up erect penises, and down open vaginas. The loser, or victim, was the player whose dice landed him or her exactly on the square in the top left-hand corner marked, *A Fate Worse Than Death?*. Surely the fate worse than death was reserved solely for those playing on level six? Surely it was?

Rosalind read on. 'First she has to remove her tights.'

'I'm not wearing any,' said Jan, while Tommy winced at the thought of what might lie ahead, and the neighbouring players glanced down at the shapely legs that stretched out from the white miniskirt she wore. Her legs were bare - no tights, no stockings; just firm, creamy-smooth thighs and calves.

'You may retain stockings and suspenders, if worn,' Rosalind read.

'They're not.'

'The instructions are now in two parts. Part One - your male partner is to pull back his chair from the table and you're to place yourself on his lap.'

Tommy had a horrible inkling of what lay in store for his attractive young wife of two years standing. He'd heard rumours of the game before.

Jan lowered herself onto Jonathan as demurely as possible, casting a quick glance at Tommy and then blushing prettily when she caught his eye. She wriggled her nicely turned bottom just once, in order to settle herself as comfortably as she could. Her short skirt had ridden almost up to the tops of her thighs, so she tugged nervously at the hem, trying to cover as much leg as possible - which wasn't very much at all.

Then she looked up at Rosalind, apprehensively waiting to learn her fate. In other circumstances, namely if they'd been alone, she'd probably have relished the opportunity to snuggle up on Jonathan's lap like this. It was rather shameful to have to admit that fact, but sometimes you had to tell yourself the truth... oh dear; Jonathan had started to rise to the occasion! She could feel him expanding powerfully against the plumpness of her right buttock...

Rosalind finished reading and looked back at her friend. 'It says here that you're to let your male partner "digitate" you in full view of everyone. For at least ten minutes, or until orgasm.'

'Digitate?' queried Jan, looking puzzled. 'What on earth is that?'

'I think it must mean finger,' Rosalind replied with a hint of a smirk.

'Oh!' gasped Jan, colouring deeply and dropping her gaze to the floor. 'Surely not. Not in front of all of you. I mean to say, surely not at all...'

Tommy couldn't believe what was happening. He couldn't believe what he was going to be forced to sit and watch. He was well aware that his closest pal fascinated Jan. He'd known that much for the past three months, ever since that wretched beach barbecue in August. He'd spent the past three months dreading what she might be prepared to let that randy sod do to her if and when they got the opportunity, and now he was going to have to sit with everyone else and actually watch Jonathan making free with the hot little honey pot she was supposed to keep only unto him!

Everyone followed Jonathan's hand with interest as it settled on bare upper thighs. The fingertips and palm pushed down between them and then began to slide slowly upward over warm, silky-smooth flesh. Tommy felt a sharp pang of jealousy as Jan automatically parted her legs to allow access to the trespassing hand. Quite what she should have done in the circumstances he wasn't certain, but he wasn't too keen on the easy manner in which she'd opened herself for his friend.

The hem of her skirt was pushed slightly back, and then most of the hand vanished from sight underneath it. Tommy, and the three others, were well aware that the fingertips would now be resting against plumply-filled knicker crotch.

Jan was too embarrassed to look at Tommy, or anyone else. Instead she closed her eyes and blushed even more deeply than ever. But her legs remained welcomingly apart. There he was, she sighed to herself. There was Jonathan, pressing lightly but firmly against her most private possession, the warmth of his fingertips making her insides tingle with pleasure. She could feel the eyes of the others riveted to the bulge of his hand beneath her skirt. She knew they knew where Jonathan was and what he was touching. But despite all that, despite the hideously embarrassing circumstances, she could feel her body appreciating that touch.

She forced herself to control her breathing as the fingertips began to rub slowly but steadily. She was determined not to let anyone know the extent to which she was being so quickly aroused.

Back and forth worked the fingertips, feeling the cleft between her thighs peeling open, feeling her juices already starting to dampen the flimsy knickers against which they were held. Back and forth worked the fingertips, relentless, remorseless, refusing to give her any respite at all. Back and forth worked the fingertips, drawing forth more oil and obliging her to strive ever harder to keep her breathing regular. Back and forth worked the fingertips until, without any conscious decision on her part, she snuggled down and rested her head on his shoulder. Back and forth worked the fingertips, until at last her breathing became noticeably heavier, despite her earlier resolve. Back and forth worked the fingertips, now slick and slippery with her natural lubrication. Back and forth worked the fingertips, making her want to cry out at the sharp pangs that seemed to be turning her tummy inside out.

'Oh,' breathed Jan, a fingertip having at last pushed inside her wet panties, and then immediately inside her. Further and further it pushed, deeper and deeper, parting her with ease. 'Oh,' she breathed again, a second finger following the first until both were buried to the knuckle. Momentarily they rested, savouring the feel of the territory they'd invaded so successfully. Savouring the texture of that which they'd taken with no resistance at all.

Jonathan's wrist had almost disappeared under the hem of the skirt; thus were all the others aware of the fact that he was now fully immersed in that delightful part of her person which female instruction card number four had ordered her make available to him.

Tommy was experiencing a weird mixture of emotions. Intense jealousy, but at the same time a certain thrill - a perverse sense of pleasure. A masochistic sense of pleasure, he decided. Derived, he supposed, from his severely wounded pride of possession. A masochistic sense of pleasure, but a very definite pleasure nevertheless.

Jan opened her eyes and gazed around, flushed in the face, misty-eyed, and not really taking in anything she saw. Then she closed them again and sighed heavily, resting her cheek on Jonathan's shoulder and waiting for what was to transpire...

Jonathan's arm drew back until the wrist re-emerged. It paused, and then was once again lost from sight as he pressed his fingers back inside her. This time the sigh from the girl was even more audible than before, and the expression on her face was one of unmistakable enjoyment. Out slid the wrist from under the skirt, back it slid again, slightly faster. Jan screwed up her eyes in confusion. She could clearly hear her juices squelching against the moving fingers, and if she could hear it so could everyone else. And the more he pushed in and out, the more she squelched. And she knew her breathing had become laboured, particularly when Jonathan's thumb was rubbing over her clitoris with every forward push.

She began to wriggle her hips and moan softly as the fingers plugged forcefully in and out. She could feel Jonathan's stiff erection pressed against her bottom, and this excited her even further. On and on went the fingering, growing in intensity while the others listened in fascination to the increased squelching sound of the fingers inside her, coupled with her moans and groans of delight.

After a while she began writhing enthusiastically against the intruding fingers. Tommy stared at the look of ecstasy on her face, recognising the expression only too well, jealous of the realisation that it wasn't, as he'd previously believed, a look she reserved for him. The squelching increased in volume and pace. Jan was replying in kind, writhing on his lap and thrusting her bottom back and forth onto the hardness of his groin. Without any conscious intent she squeezed a hand between them, cupping his substantial erection through his trousers and then squeezing in time with the push of his fingers inside her.

The hem of her skirt was pushed back with the power and speed of the frigging, revealing glistening fingers driving in and out of displaced pink panties. Now everyone could see as well as hear the remorseless way in which she was being probed. Tommy winced and groaned inwardly with a strange combination of pain and desire. He wanted to cover his ears and look away, but found his eyes riveted in fascination to the sight of his wife being masturbated in full view of himself and his friends.

'Come on, Jan,' Jonathan crooned with encouragement, feeling her insides starting to spasm. 'Come on, baby, you can do it. Just let it happen.'

'Ooohhhh!' she squealed, jerking her head back and staring wide-eyed at the ceiling.

'That's it, baby,' he urged. 'That's the way.'

'Oh, Jonathan...' she burbled, 'Jonathan... you're making me come so hard. That's just so *good*...'

'I wish it was my dick,' he whispered in her ear, 'instead of my fingers.'

'So do I,' she sighed, oblivious to her surroundings. 'Oh, so do I...'

A few minutes later Jan was still sitting on Jonathan's lap, red of face and short of breath. She glanced down at her thighs and hurriedly pulled her skirt back over the 'V' of pink knickers that had become exposed to all.

What on earth must she have looked like when sitting there with her legs wide open and Jonathan's fingers working away like mad between them? Oh, how horribly embarrassing!

'Now for part two of the forfeit,' announced Rosalind.

'Surely th-that's enough?' stammered Jan. 'I've done my bit. Can't someone else have a go?'

'Rules are rules,' replied Rosalind, carefully reading the instruction card she held in her hand. 'You lost the game, so you must pay the price... and you'll like this,' she added gleefully. 'A sound bare-bottom spanking, it says here. At the hands of your good husband.'

'Oh, no,' Jan gasped in alarm, never having been spanked before, but Rosalind ignored her protest and continued.

'But first we have to take a vote on whether she deserves it or not. Hands up all those who think she's just enjoyed herself far more than she should and ought to pay the price?'

All hands lifted into the air, Tommy's being the first. Revenge, he thought to himself; revenge for the bittersweet torment he'd had to suffer over the past ten minutes or so. How often he'd stared at her naked or lightly knickered bottom and fantasised about spanking it!

'Good,' Rosalind concluded, 'so that decides it. You're to rest yourself over your husband's lap and accept a vigorous spanking.'

Following Rosalind's continuing instructions, Tommy moved his chair into the middle of the room so everyone would get a good view. Jan stood beside him; trim and leggy in her short skirt and high heels.

'This is the game plan,' Rosalind said, reading from the instruction card. 'You are a wronged husband. Your wife has been unfaithful and you've just found her out. You're angry and you're to punish her accordingly in the manner already stated. No mercy is to be shown.'

'Oh dear,' Jan whispered, not looking him, or anyone else, in the eye.

'Bend over my knee,' Tommy demanded firmly, thrilling anticipation having rushed straight to his groin. She reddened but didn't say or do anything. 'I said bend over my knee,' he repeated.

'You're going to hurt me...'

'He certainly is,' Rosalind cut in. 'We've all seen how much you've earned it.'

'But I only did what the card told me to do.'

'And now it's telling you to do this,' replied Rosalind.

'Bend over my knee,' repeated Tommy.

'Do I really have to?'

'Yes,' confirmed several of the others.

She gave a sigh of resignation and then slowly, and very reluctantly, she began to comply. 'This isn't at all easy,' she muttered unhappily, as her head approached the floor and her white miniskirt rode to the tops of her thighs, just revealing her tiny pink knickers, the seat of which was stretched across the much-admired part of Tommy's wife that she was now tilting up at him so temptingly.

Tommy ran the palm of a hand slowly back and forth over the swell of her buttocks, enjoying the anticipation along with everyone else... except Jan. Then, purposefully, he held the hem of her skirt in his free hand, and paused for dramatic effect. Jan groaned inwardly, lying over her husband's lap as she waited for him to expose her to public scrutiny.

He decided to make her wait a while longer, while the others sat eagerly, looking forward to what was to follow.

At length Tommy made his move, turning up the hem of her tiny skirt until it was folded onto the small of her back, thereby affording everyone a full, unrestricted view of saucy plump cheeks sweetly decorated with a minuscule pair of tight pink knickers, so small that they really did no more than highlight the delightful curves and contours to which they clung.

'Yes, very nice,' someone murmured after Tommy's hand had slipped inside the knickers and slid them all the way down to her ankles, thus revealing two globes of pale perfection.

Tommy stared down at the gorgeous bottom draped over his lap so appealingly. It seemed to peep nervously back at him, blushing with embarrassment. 'Yes, very nice indeed,' he concurred, with husbandly pride.

Not that he intended to show it any mercy. Against the back of his hand he'd felt that the crotch of her panties was soaked right through from her experience with Jonathan; a fact that strengthened his resolve to execute the game plan to the very letter of the law.

Jan lay over his knee in sweet surrender, naked below the waist, her hands and toes on the carpet. She groaned silently in despair. Could anyone ever have felt more vulnerable? She closed her eyes and tried to pretend that she and Tommy were on their own. But she could sense the gaze of the others all over her naked bottom. At the same time she could sense her husband's right hand above his head, powerful and uncompromising. She took a deep breath and waited, fearful but submissive, for the first swat across her upturned cheeks.

She didn't have to wait long. Suddenly, and with considerable venom, he delivered a perfect handprint across the centre of her right cheek. Then he painted a second, overlapping the first. Then a third, a fourth, a fifth, and a sixth.

The process was repeated on the other buttock, then without pausing to admire his handiwork he began to spank each cheek in turn, before realising that the constant and repeated application of his hand on the same area of flesh caused much more discomfort than assaulting one buttock after the other. So he lay twenty stinging slaps in quick succession on one side, and then another twenty on the other, and it was clear from her heightened agitation that this was the way to proceed.

The six non-participants stared avidly at the scene in front of them, the men fervently wishing they were involved, the women hugely relieved they were not. Rosalind in particular was relishing the situation. Each loud smack was a sheer delight. Everyone knew Jan was desperate for Jonathan to shag her, probably even Tommy, so this was poetic justice at its very best. This would teach her a thing or two. It was a pity she and Jonathan had to see so much of the little viper. But Tommy and Jonathan were so pally it couldn't be helped.

Oh, how lovely, the way in which Jan was in such obvious torment. The way in which she was sobbing and writhing her bottom from side to side as if to gain some sort of relief. The same bottom she was longing to slide naked into bed beside her husband's best mate! Well, the little witch was certainly getting her just rewards in the most appropriate of ways!

The instruction card had said nothing about a spanking, of course. It was just a shame for Jan that Rosalind made that bit up!

It really ought to have been her own bottom under attack, Jennie thought as Tommy's hand continued to rise and fall at speed, not poor Jan's. She really ought to have been strong enough not to do what Jonathan had asked. Perhaps she could blame the wine. What was she going to tell Michael when they got home? That they'd just had a bit of a kiss and a cuddle, she supposed. Just a bit of innocent groping and nothing more. Thank heavens nothing had oozed from the corners of her mouth and dripped onto her blouse, where the stains would be plain for all to see...

Just over an hour later Jan stood in her bedroom, ruefully inspecting her burning buttocks in the full-length mirror behind her. 'Look what you've done to me,' she pouted. 'How could you do that to my bottom?'

'Don't you think you deserved it, letting Jonathan bring you off like that with all of us sitting watching?'

'It wasn't my fault. I couldn't help it. It just happened.'

'It wouldn't have happened if you'd been hating every moment. It wouldn't have happened if you didn't fancy him, would it?'

'I suppose not.'

'You told him you wished he was fucking you.'

'D-did I?' she stammered, blushing fiercely.

'Yes, you did.'

'I'm sorry.'

'How do you feel now?'

'Sore. Hot and sore. You can see that much for yourself. Just look at the colour of my poor bum. Especially here and here.' She swivelled her hips in the mirror in order to display the dark discoloration on the roundest part of each fiery red cheek.

'And what else do you feel?'

'Hideously embarrassed. How am I ever going to be able to look any of them in the face again, after what they've watched Jonathan do to me? And then you...'

Tommy ignored the question. 'Do you feel anything else as well?'

At length she replied. 'Well, yes... very, very sexy...'

'So do I,' he said. Spanking his wife's lovely bottom in front of other people had turned him on more than he'd ever thought possible. He felt so proud of her as she'd been lying there head down over his knee, weeping softly, her hair sweeping the floor, and those smooth, pouting cheeks bouncing and blushing more and more prettily with each stinging crack from the palm of his hand.

He stared at the delightful reflection in the mirror, watching her hands slowly and carefully massaging her stricken parts, his bloated erection aching for release. 'Let's get into bed and do something about it?' he croaked. 'Let's proceed directly to level six.'

She saw the direction of his gaze in the mirror and wriggled her hips provocatively. 'You'll have to let me lie on top, darling,' she giggled wickedly. 'And keep your hands to yourself.'

'I can't guarantee that,' he replied, eagerly unfastening his trousers.

She stared in amazement at the shape thrusting upward and stretching his boxer shorts. 'Mmmmm...' she purred, a mischievous twinkle in her eye, 'where did you get that monster from? This isn't going to be level six... more like level twenty-six!'

BOOK TWO - ACCIDENTS WILL HAPPEN
Author's Note

Hi. I'm Alison North. Now that I've finished telling you how Jennie and three of my other girlfriends have suffered at the hands - and other devices - of various third parties, I thought you might like to hear of my own unfortunate experiences. I've not been able to bring myself to detail the first time I was OTK, because of my total aversion to that particular ex-boyfriend. So here's an accurate account of the four occasions since then that I've been subjected to extremely painful consequences.

Chapter Seven - Alison's Christmas Stocking Filler

It's widely accepted amongst office workers that Christmas doesn't count. Christmas coitus, I mean to say. Ask any respectably married lady who's held such a job for more than a couple of years and she'll readily agree with me when I tell you that getting yourself dicked by a co-employee on the afternoon of Christmas Eve doesn't mean you've been unfaithful to your husband or boyfriend. You've only done exactly the same as thousands of other ladies in office blocks up and down the length and breadth of the country. At least, that's what you say to yourself as you stand there, your smart black skirt round your waist, pulling your filmy little knickers up past your lace-topped stockings and matching suspenders. That's what you say to yourself as you stand adjusting your knickers and watching your colleague from marketing tucking his sticky, slowly shrinking penis back into his boxer shorts.

And that's not all you say to yourself. No, you tell yourself firmly: you will not be consumed with guilt when you return home to hearth and husband. You will not suffer any form of guilty conscience whatsoever, because, as everyone knows in the City, and beyond, the hours of three to five p.m. on Christmas Eve were created solely for the purpose of intoxicated fornication, and absolutely nothing else at all. Not only is it accepted, it's fully expected. It's the traditional way of starting the Christmas break. The mince pies on Christmas morning just wouldn't taste the same without it.

I'd always fancied George from sales. George, with his black hair and laughing blue eyes. I'd noticed him the first morning I started working there. The crotch of my little g-string knickers had been soaked in a matter of seconds. But I'd no intention of making a play for him. After all, I'd only married my absolute angel of a Michael just over a week beforehand. But that didn't mean, of course, that I couldn't get all hot and bothered at the sight of another man. Another virile young man who I could tell at a glance was just my type.

Five months ticked steadily by, during which time I got to know George quite well. And the better I knew him, the damper my panties were when he was around. I liked the way he always wore a crisp white shirt and pale blue tie. The shirt emphasised the fact that his face was tanned to a light golden brown. It was always a fitted shirt displaying broad shoulders and chest, and a flat stomach to perfection. And his hips were so beautifully slim. I could have sat forever and watched him ploughing back and forth across our floor - the sixth floor wherein sales and marketing are housed. There were plenty of other attractive men, both young and not so young, but George was someone special. Very quickly I acquired the habit of carrying a spare pair of knickers to work. And most days I left the office wishing I'd brought a third.

I can remember that first Christmas just as if it was yesterday - which, in fact, is exactly when it was, since I'm lying here on Christmas morning being screwed by my own dear Michael. Fortunately he can't get into my mind as easily as he can my pussy!

The alcohol had started to flow in the pub at lunchtime. Then vast quantities of it, in bottled form, were carried back to work at two o'clock. For a further sixty minutes the phones were manned, rather badly, and reception still functioned, just about. Then the office closed officially and the serious drinking began behind locked doors. We in technical servicing reckoned it took my best friend, Jennie Jamieson from marketing, less than four minutes before she disappeared with her immediate boss, his hand cupped to the seat of her skirt as they went.

'What are you doing for Christmas?' I asked George, who was perched on the table opposite, whisky in hand.

'Changing fiancées,' he replied with a sexy grin. 'On New Year's Eve, he continued. 'Out with the old and in with the new.'

'George!' the five or six girls in my circle gasped as one. 'What an awful sort of thing to say!'

'Well, I'm an awful sort of person,' he said happily.

And so the boozing and bantering continued, and with my eyes constantly returning to George I could feel my juices seeping down my thighs. My tiny pink knickers had finally given up the struggle to contain. Jim, my sort of superior, placed a hand on my knee. 'You look great in such a sexy skirt,' he said rather thickly.

'I always wear sexy skirts,' I pointed out, not attempting to remove his hand but wishing it belonged to George instead. 'And high heels,' I added for good measure.

'And no knickers,' he murmured, lowering his head and peering drunkenly up my skirt. 'None that I can see, anyway.'

'They're pink,' I giggled indignantly, blushing as he continued to stare at my crotch.

'You're looking at pink panties, not pink pussy,' George informed him. 'I think you're pissed, old man.'

George wandered off in the direction of the photocopying room, where the remaining bottles of booze were stored. Jim let go of my knee and lurched after him, towards the kitchen to make a coffee, I thought I heard him slur. I drained my glass with a single gulp and poured another, and then took a hefty swig of that. For some reason George's reference to 'pink pussy' had really made me excited. Did he know that every morning I used a special cream that made it as smooth and hairless as a baby's bottom? No, of course he didn't. But he might well have guessed that it was open and glistening as I sat there opposite him, thinking all sorts of naughty thoughts...

I finished my drink and got to my feet. I'd made a decision, and George's virtue was definitely under threat. I'd follow him through to the photocopying room and see if anything big could be made to come up. After all, it was only Christmas. It didn't really count. It didn't mean I loved Michael any the less.

Walking away from the merry gathering I could sense the eyes of the men glued to the well-filled seat of my skirt as it swished sexily from side to side. I blushed again. Did they suspect my lecherous intentions? I rather thought that they probably did.

That morning I'd deliberately dressed to please George. My short skirt and high heels were black. Everything else was pink, from my silk blouse all the way down to the toes of my stockings. I knew he approved of those colours on a girl. I was particularly pleased with my minuscule bra and panty set and the way it matched my lace stocking tops and suspenders. I'm trying not to be immodest when I say that I definitely have the figure to go with such delicious lingerie. Had I hoped, as I slipped into them in front of my husband, that George would have the opportunity to appreciate the frothy little garments? I'll leave you to be the judge of that.

I opened the door to the copying room very quietly. The main light was off, but in the grey light from the window I could see George with his back to me, working at the photocopier. Silently I closed the door and turned the key. Then I crept across the room until I was directly behind him. I wrapped both arms tightly around his chest. 'Don't turn round,' I whispered, dropping my hands to his crotch and snuggling against him so he could feel my boobs pressing into his back and my groin into his buttocks. I cupped my left hand under his testicles and used my right to massage him just above. Instantly he started to stir and stiffen under my touch. Within a few seconds he was fully upright and as hard as any respectably married young lady could have wished. I ran my palm up and down the full length of the enlivened part of his person. It felt very promising indeed. Exactly the size I'd always thought George would be. No one as hunky as he could fail to be handsomely hung.

'Guess who it is,' I giggled. 'I'm tall. I've got wavy blonde hair, my first name is Alison, and my husband's surname is North.' I squeezed him tenderly with both hands, thrilling at the heat and power I could feel inside his bulging trouser front. 'Is that enough clues?'

'I guess so,' George said as he turned to face me... only it wasn't George at all. It was Jim, my sort of superior, looking very unlike George now I could see his face, despite the crisp white shirt he was wearing. As his hands settled firmly on my bottom I buried my face in his chest in order to hide my shock and consternation. His hot cock was now thrust hard against my stomach, and I could feel it pulsing in anticipation while he massaged my bum with evident enthusiasm. It was a tricky situation. There I was, having thrust my favours upon him thinking he was dishy George. There I was, my face a picture of embarrassment at finding he was only the pretty ordinary Jim. I ask you now, what on earth should I have done? What action should I have taken? It wasn't easy, but I decided my first priority was to conceal my surprise and embarrassment, but I couldn't hide my face against his chest forever. I needed to do something else while I recovered my composure...

So I sank to my knees in front of him and reached for his zip. It was a fair compromise, my tipsy brain thought at the time. After all, it isn't adultery, is it?

Seconds later his trousers and pants were around his ankles, and his sturdy prick was sliding steadily in and out of my mouth as I gave him head to the best of my ability - which, even if I say so myself, is not inconsiderable. In fact rather the opposite, I've always been told.

Up and down I worked my head, taking almost all of him into my mouth and throat, and then sucking hard at the round, plum-coloured tip each time I drew back. I have to admit that he possessed a most appetising taste, even though he was only Jim. And he was so hot that I could almost imagine he was scalding my lips and tongue. I cradled his balls in the palm of my hand and felt they were heavy with fluid. This wasn't so bad, I said to myself. There were worse ways of passing the afternoon, even if he wasn't George. He had a really nice cock and it felt very right in my mouth.

It didn't take long. The first boiling jet stream shot down my throat soon after I'd started. I pulled back my head and allowed him to splatter my lips and chin. I always love to do that. Then I swallowed him again, savouring the lovely flavour of the liquid swirling over my tongue and down my throat. It seemed to last for ages. Greedily I gobbled, wondering if the well would ever run dry. He cradled my head in his hands and continued to ejaculate with a ferocity I found hard to believe.

But at last he was spent. 'Damn, that was good!' he groaned, as I felt him slowly starting to contract in my mouth. 'I always thought you fancied George, not me.'

'Not really,' I mumbled indistinctly, because he was still a considerable size.

'Let's do it on the photocopier,' he breathed hotly, just as I removed his still quite substantial presence from between my lips. I looked at the huge QX4DL. It was more like a laboratory bench than a copying machine. But that was because it was an industrial colour-copier with so many advanced functions it made your head spin to use it.

'You've only just finished,' I demurred, but that was not a problem, I realised as he started to swell again right in front of my eyes. With a sigh of resignation I got to my feet, pulling my skirt up to my waist and then daintily stepping out of my knickers. It was still Christmas, I reminded myself as I lay on my back, my bottom resting on the opaque plastic upon which the documents to be copied are placed. It was hard and unyielding, but I'm very nicely upholstered in my postern department, as my husband is always so pleased to point out.

Jim mounted me in the good old-fashioned missionary position, his dick as eager and erect as when it was in my mouth, and although it was the wrong man on the end of that dick, I found I was as open and ready for him as I could possibly be.

For the next fifteen minutes he fucked me for all he was worth - almost as if his life depended upon it. And I have to admit that I responded in kind, writhing like a snake while he pounded and probed. As we climaxed together there came a blinding flash of light, but it was nothing spiritual, just my right hand accidentally activating the copier as I thrashed wildly from side to side in delight.

I slithered myself free from his still-invasive presence and stood up, somewhat unsteadily, turning round to look for my discarded pink panties. 'Gotcha!' he growled, slapping playfully but firmly my sticky bare bottom, which I'd foolishly left within range. Then he reached out with both hands. 'What a bum!' he added coarsely, before digging in his thumbs and fingertips as hard as he could. With a yelp I leapt away. Mind you, I'm well used to that sort of mistreatment from Michael. He says it's simply the price a girl has to pay for having far too gorgeous a bum. Which is rather nice, I suppose, in a way...

I wriggled back into my knickers and smoothed down my skirt. 'You stay here for a while,' Jim said as he unlocked the door. 'You don't want to be seen leaving with me.'

Jim opened the door and walked out, and as he did so George strode in, looking somewhat less than delighted.

Jim was gone, whistling tunelessly but cheerfully as he went, leaving me alone in the room with the fabulous George - red-faced and outdone by his rival from marketing. Not quite the circumstances I'd have preferred.

'What have you two been up to?' he demanded, clearly full of suspicion.

I stared down at the floor in dismay and embarrassment, feeling Jim's warm, sticky juices starting to seep into my panties. 'N-nothing,' I stammered unhappily, doubting whether he'd believe me. 'Nothing at all.'

'Don't give me that,' he snapped. 'The door was locked. What the hell have you been doing with Jim?'

'Nothing, George.'

'I was expecting you to follow me through to the kitchen.'

'I did. I mean, I was. I mean, I thought you were coming here. I thought Jim said he was going to the kitchen. I thought he said he was going there to make coffee.'

'Don't lie to me,' he said impatiently. 'Jim said he was coming here to make a copy. I was in the kitchen waiting for you to join me.'

'Oh, I thought he said he was going to make a coffee, not a copy.'

'Liar,' he sulked.

'George, that's unfair.'

'Instead of joining me you come in here and fuck that bloody Jim Browne.'

'I didn't,' I said rather feebly.

'Of course you did.'

'George...'

'Hey, what's that?' he said, pointing to the out tray of the huge industrial copier upon which I'd so recently been laid. 'What is that?' he repeated.

He picked up a colourful two-foot square sheet of copying paper and held it out for us both to inspect. Then he flicked on the overhead light so we could see more clearly, whereupon I turned an even brighter shade of beetroot and nearly died of shame. There, on the photocopy I'd accidentally made during my orgasm, was the perfect photo-print of my blushing bare bottom, just as clear as it could possibly have been; a perfect photo of the twin cheeks of my bum on top of the machine. And not only that. There, also, was the very clear picture of Jim's rampant cock, halfway in and halfway out. Long and thick it was, and clearly disappearing inside my pussy. George was holding the perfect reproduction of my adulterous rear and pussy well and truly caught on the job.

The quality of the photo was so good that you could even see every detail of the tiny butterfly tattoo adorning my left cheek. The one Michael loves so much, and the one my family and friends would recognise instantly as I always wear a thong on beach holidays, rather than bikini bottoms.

George stared long and hard at the picture. 'Fucked on the photocopier!' he exclaimed at length, gritting his teeth in jealous frustration. 'You're supposed to fancy me, not Jim Browne.'

'I did,' I admitted, seeing another side to the sulky individual, 'but I'm rapidly changing my mind about that.'

'You're supposed to be my piece of Christmas totty, not his,' he went on, rather presumptuously for my liking.

'Who said that?' I demanded.

'I did. Didn't you hear me?'

'I might have been intending to be your piece of Christmas *totty* - as you put it - but I'm certainly not now. Go and get stuffed, George.'

'That's charming,' he snapped unfairly. 'You tell me to go and get stuffed after you've just chosen to get stuffed by Jim Browne rather than me.'

'That's got nothing to do with you. I might have fancied you once but that's all changed. I wouldn't let you touch me now.'

He grabbed my left wrist. 'Well, we'll see about that.'

'George, let go. You're hurting me.'

'I'm going to hurt you a great deal more than that.'

'George, let go!'

'I'm going to teach your randy little arse a lesson it'll never forget.'

'Oh no you're not,' I insisted. 'As I just said, it's got nothing to do with you.'

'Fucking Jim Browne has everything to do with me.'

'It certainly does not,' I challenged indignantly.

'Do you want everyone under the sun to know what you've been doing with Jim?'

'Um, no...'

'Do you want everyone to see this picture of Jim's dick stuck inside you?'

I shook my head, a bad feeling looming.

'Do you want me to e-mail it to Michael and everyone else on your contacts list right now, with a full explanation?'

I shook my head again, defeat imminent.

'So bend over the copying machine.'

'You're serious about this, aren't you?'

'I am,' he confirmed smugly, 'deadly serious.'

I could see in his face that he meant every word. It was entirely obvious to me. I was left in no doubt as to what he would do if I refused to comply. 'You'll give me that copy if I do as you say?' I asked.

'Yes.'

'And you'll keep quiet about all this?'

'Yes.'

'How do I know I can trust you?'

'You don't. But what other choice do you have?'

It was a very fair question. Unfortunately. What other choice did I have? And it wasn't as if I was totally without blame, was it? I'd just been unfaithful to my lovely Michael, hadn't I? I'd allowed my lust for George to lead me into committing adultery, hadn't I? And in addition I could now see for myself how ill-directed that lust had been. George was in no way the person I'd always thought him to be. Much the opposite, in fact - he was a bit of a manipulative rat.

So I'd allowed myself to cuckold my absolute angel of a husband with someone I didn't really want because of my lust for someone else whom I now discovered I didn't actually like at all. If anyone deserved what George was proposing to do, then I guess it must have been me. That was some sort of consolation, I told myself, as I stood there facing the photocopying machine, trying to get my mind round what was going to happen. Perhaps a sound spanking would help to ease the guilt I was starting to feel.

'Pull up your skirt and bend over the photocopier,' he ordered, looking infuriatingly triumphant. 'Elbows on the top,' he added.

This I did, blushing furiously, but George didn't allow me to dwell on my embarrassment for long. My knickers, now somewhat soggy, were slipped down to my feet in a trice, and immediately the chastisement began.

'You've been lying to me,' he muttered, slapping my right buttock and making me shriek in protest. 'You always intended to fuck him instead of me.'

'I didn't,' I gasped, as he slapped me again. 'Not that it's any concern of yours.'

'You're nothing but a prick-teaser.'

'I'm not. I came in here looking for you... ouch!'

He slapped me again, three times in a row, making me gasp and squeal. 'You thought he said he was going to make coffee, not a copy?'

'Ouch! Yes, I did... ouch! Ouch!'

'Do you expect me to believe that?'

'I don't give a monkey's what you... ouch! Ouch! Ouch! You rotten sod!'

He made no further comment, but continued his assault on my right buttock with all his might. The pain brought tears to my eyes, as well as warm, slippery oil to my vagina. Now I was doubly lubricated, the residue of Jim Browne mingling with my own juices.

After what seemed an age he turned his attention to the other cheek, very rapidly warming it up to the same degree as the right. Without relent he spanked my poor bottom as hard as he could, while I sobbed and cringed.

And all the time I could sense his eyes all over me, all over the cheeks of my rapidly overheating rear, as they quivered and coloured with every stinging slap. Cheeks that were framed with the lacy pink suspenders and stocking tops I'd been so happy to put on that morning. It occurred to me that my poor bottom would now be a much brighter colour than the lingerie surrounding it. Teardrops dripped onto the surface of the photocopier as I wept and wailed and wriggled and writhed my hips in discomfort. I'd forgotten all about the cumulative effect of a hand landing heavily on the same part of the same buttock time after time after time. Each slap seems to hurt twice as much as the one before; until you begin to wonder how much longer you'll be able to endure it.

But I did endure it. I stood there sobbing, yet letting him spank me to his heart's content. It helped a bit to remind myself just how much I'd earned the punishment; just how much I deserved all the hurt. But even so it was a considerable ordeal, and I can remember the relief each time he switched from one cheek to the other. It was short-lived, however, for very soon that other cheek was suffering the same ever-increasing pain...

I rested my forehead on the copying machine, sobbing uncontrollably as George's hand cracked down again and again. Each slap sounded like a report from a pistol as it echoed around the room, while I just stood there, bent over the machine, tears squeezing from my eyes while his hand beat twenty or so times against one cheek, and then the other.

'Are you still telling me you weren't looking for Jim?' he demanded, after an eternity of non-stop torture.

'Yes,' I snuffled, the punishment starting again.

'You were looking for me?'

'Y-yes.'

He switched to my left cheek. 'Why did you fuck him, then?'

I closed my eyes, but this didn't stem the tears. 'I don't know.'

The assault on my left buttock continued unabated. 'Well, if you don't know I can't imagine who might.'

'It just happened... I don't know why... but it's got nothing to do with you, George.'

'Well, I'm making it my business,' was all he'd say as the spanking raged on and on... and even further on.

I tried to think about my lovely Michael in an effort to distract myself from the pain. I tried to imagine that he was the one standing there behind me, slapping my bum for all he was worth. That did seem to help for a while. I was even starting to feel a bit sexy at the thought of my own husband sorting me out for the way I'd just cheated on him, but then the spell was broken and it was only the dastardly George once again.

Suddenly I heard the door open behind me. George placed a restraining hand on my back. 'Stay still,' he warned me, still slapping lustily. I groaned inwardly with dismay.

'Good grief!' I heard someone exclaim. I turned my head and looked back, blushing all the way down to my high-heeled shoes. It was Tony from accounts, and a girl from reception who stood there holding a smart pair of navy blue trousers in her hand and wearing nothing below the waist but small black knickers and shoes. I still have difficulty trying to figure that one out.

'Don't be concerned,' George said to them, slapping my left buttock. 'Mrs North and I are just discussing the rather thorny question of sexual promiscuity in a working environment.'

'That sounds quite an interesting topic,' said Tony, making the girl giggle.

'It is,' agreed George, slapping as forcefully as ever. 'And as you can tell it's been quite a heated debate.'

'Yes, I can see that for myself. Very clearly indeed.'

The girl in the small black knickers giggled again. 'So can I.'

'You'll excuse me if I continue with the discussion?' asked George.

'Of course.'

I blushed even more. The situation was almost as embarrassing as it was painful. My bare bottom being spanked by a work colleague was bad enough, but having two others standing there watching him do it?

'Doesn't that look so horny,' the girl breathed after a while, George's hand still cracking down with monotonous regularity. 'Come on, Tony, let's go to the ladies' cloakroom.'

The door closed behind them, and I sighed with relief.

Just as I decided I simply couldn't take any more, whatever the consequences, the spanking stopped and he placed a palm on each cheek, presumably to check the heat for himself. 'I think that's about right,' he said. 'You seem to be done to a turn.'

I most certainly was. My bottom was even hotter and sorer than when that awful Tim Reynolds had put me over his knee all those years before. But at least the tears dried up almost as soon as the slapping ceased.

And then, oh dear, suddenly I realised how wicked and turned on I felt. Never had I known such rabid arousal coursing through my body. Behind my back I heard the very familiar sound of a zip fastener urgently parting company with itself. I twisted my head and peered back over my shoulder. I could see at once that his cock was standing rigidly up to attention, just an inch or so from the cheeks of my blistered bottom, and he was every bit as generously endowed as I'd always suspected he might be.

'In your dreams,' I fully intended to tell him, but to my eternal shame it came out as, '*Oh, yes please.*'

Chapter Eight - Alison in the Dark

So I've told you how George's hand set fire to the cheeks of my naughty bottom in the photocopying room last Christmas. It was only the second time it had ever been done to me, but in the end it proved slightly more acceptable than the first, when that awful Tim Reynolds took offence at the way I scratched the bumper on his beaten-up old Ford Anglia. I'm sure he just used that as an excuse to do what he'd always wanted to do to me. Anyway, now I'm going to tell you about the third time I was made to suffer in that way... and why.

I swear I don't know how it happened. And so does Jennie. Not that it's doing us much good at the moment, as you can judge when I tell you that the two of us are standing here in the corner of the bedroom, facing the wall in disgrace, whilst trying to soothe our totally naked bottoms with our hands. We dare not even look back over our shoulders at our husbands, in case they implement their threat to put us back across their knees and punish us all over again. We don't fancy that at all. It wasn't the least bit erotic, just very painful and humiliating. I've lost track of how long we were both draped there, opposite each other on the edge of each single bed, protesting as one scalding slap after another rained down on our upturned flanks. The harder Michael spanked me the harder and faster Jennie got her own unjust desserts. And the more I howled the more she followed suit, our buttocks turning an ever-darkening shade of red as time ticked remorselessly by.

And now we've been allowed to our feet at long last, we find we have to stand in this rotten corner, our faces tearstained and our poor, sore bottoms bruised and bare to their angry gaze. It's so embarrassing! I mean, it would be okay if it was just my Michael, I suppose. And I guess Jennie wouldn't mind too much if it was only her husband glaring at her from behind. But when they're both sitting there, staring at us, fuming with rage...

God, my cheeks are really on fire! And if I glance surreptitiously to my left I can see that Jennie is in exactly the same state. No matter how much we try to comfort ourselves with our hands, the burning just seems to get worse. And having our infuriated tormentors sitting on the bed behind us, discussing a repeat performance, only serves to make everything worse.

Our spouses still think it was deliberate, you see. Well, as if either Jennie or I were that sort of a girl. We're respectably married young ladies who're both in love with our husbands, even if once or twice in the past circumstances may have conspired against us. Well I mean, it happens, doesn't it?

Oh dear, I suppose I'd better start at the beginning instead of the end. Well, Michael and I were on a walking holiday with our friends Jennie and Michael Jamieson, staying at a youth hostel right in the middle of nowhere. Or rather, right in the middle of Cumbria. The weather was idyllic, and so was the scenery. The only slight drawback was the hostel's insistence on adhering to their old-fashioned rules, which meant there were separate rooms for men and women, and no married quarters whatsoever. And for two young couples still in the early stages of wedded bliss this was, of course, quite unthinkable. Not a day had passed since our marriage when I'd failed to make love to Michael in one way or another. And I know Jennie is just the same. I know she hasn't missed a day either. She and her own Michael are at it like stoats whenever and wherever they can - as you're about to find out...

Jennie and I are so alike we're often mistaken for sisters. Alike in looks as well as in everything else, with blonde hair and the sort of figure that turns countless heads. I suppose we sort of encourage the attention, wearing short skirts and nicely fitted tops, I mean. Well, there's no harm in that, is there? Provided you have every intention of staying safely inside them. Just because a man is able to admire the shape of your bottom through a pair of skin-tight jeans, it doesn't mean you're obliged to slide it between his sheets, now does it? He really doesn't have any right to mooch about bemoaning what he's missing out on, does he?

'Separate rooms?' gasped Jennie, staring in disbelief at the fierce-looking woman apparently in charge of the hostel. 'But we've been married for nearly a year.'

'Separate rooms,' snapped the dragon, refusing to hear another word about our very natural desire to partake of our conjugal rights whenever we chose.

After a boatload of booze at the nearby pub, we returned to the hostel and said our reluctant goodnights to the boys. The third bunk in our room was empty, so at least Jennie and I were able to cuddle together in one bed to console each other about the loss of our men.

Then I kissed her, and she responded fiercely with her hot little tongue, making me feel randier than ever. After a while I pulled back the covers and gently turned her onto her front, wanting to be able to watch myself fondling the cheeks of her pretty bottom.

'Your bum is so sexy,' I giggled, before slipping two fingers into her lovely little pussy. 'It always turns me on.' As she wriggled her hips from side to side in appreciation, I began to finger-fuck her, just as we'd done to each other on occasions in the past when boyfriends or fiancés had been conspicuous by their absence.

'That's nice, Allie,' she murmured, as I probed her slowly but deeply. She was incredibly hot and wet. 'Oooh,' she moaned at length, starting to orgasm so sweetly I wanted to die for her.

'I wish I was a man,' I sighed wistfully. 'I'd fuck you all night long.'

For the next ten minutes Jennie's fingers were in my sex and my bum, and her tongue was deep in my mouth, making me gasp and groan. It was just as well that the hostel was nearly empty, and that the dragon hung out on the far side of the building from our room.

Eventually I lifted my head and stared into her face. 'This is only making me randier,' I groaned, as she continued to probe and please.

'I know,' she murmured. 'It's lovely, but it's just making me long for Mike's cock.'

'Let's go and find our husband's,' I urged. 'Bugger the rules of the house.'

It was a really sexy experience, lying in the dark, three or four feet apart, listening to each other being screwed by our respective spouses.

In the very faint glimmer of electric light through the window, I stared to my right in delight at the picture of Jennie's spectacular bottom rising and falling over the groin of her special man. And I expect she felt the same glow of pleasure when I then slipped on top of my husband and shagged him as hard as I could.

Then Jennie was facedown, and I could hear her Michael's loins smacking into her buttocks as he plumbed every inch she had to offer. I knew my own Michael was listening too as I squeezed him with my internal muscles, and felt him start to flood my womb for the second time that night. Together we lay there, with me still on top, sharing the erotic pleasure of listening to Jennie being seriously sorted out right at our side.

Half an hour later we slipped stealthily back to our room, skimpy little undies in hand, and spent the rest of the night in my rather undersized bed, curled up together on our sides like spoons.

We were high in the hills, miles from anywhere and miles from anyone else. All morning I'd been thinking about how we'd spent the previous night. About making love to my husband while Jennie and her own fella were also at it. We sat on the lush grass looking down on Lake Buttermere as it shimmered in the August sunshine. I wrapped my arms round my own Michael and kissed him passionately, and slowly ran a hand from his chest down to the crotch of his jeans, and as I expected, he was fully erect by the time I arrived.

I glanced to one side and caught Jennie's eye. She smiled, and I knew we were both thinking the same sexy thoughts. Then she began to fondle her husband, pushing a hand down inside the front of his trousers as he stretched back on the grass, and soon the four of us were naked, Jennie and I lying side by side while our partners worked away between our legs with long, steady strokes that made us shiver and sigh.

I found it incredibly sensual, lying there with Michael yet able to watch the other two as well. And I know they felt the same. We made no attempt to disguise our interest in each other - much the opposite, in fact.

I stared at Jennie and her Michael, loving the sight of his tool, glistening wet with her juices, slipping smoothly back and forth inside her sweet little pussy. I loved the way he was tenderly chewing her nipples, while at the same time cupping and squeezing her buttocks in both hands. But even more than that, I loved the knowledge that they were enjoying the spectacle of me underneath Michael, taking his gloriously erect dick. It was like being made love to several times over. Not only were Michael and I loving each other so beautifully, but it felt as if he and I were also participating in the other couple's pleasure, and further, that they were doing the same with ours. It was a really gorgeous sensation. Very quickly my climax was upon me and I stared wide-eyed at Jennie, wanting her to see how exquisitely my lovely fella was making me come...

Michael encouraged me on top of him, wanting the others to be able to admire the cheeks of my bottom, I'm sure. He's exceptionally proud of that particular part of my person, I'm totally delighted to say.

After a while Jennie followed suit, allowing me to gaze with pleasure at her perfect bottom as it moved gracefully up and down. Allowing me to gaze with pleasure at those saucy twin peaks as she rode the full length of her husband's stalk. I don't know why, but it's a fact that most girls are just as enthusiastic as any man about a pair of shapely female buttocks, and I think I've made it plain that both Jennie and I are in pretty good shape in that department.

So we screwed our men in unison - in very much the way they'd been doing us - all four of us savouring the really horny feeling of doing it with your partner, while at the same time watching and being watched by someone else. A triple thrill, you have to admit.

'Oh, Mikey...' Jennie sighed happily, the stout column on which she was riding having finally brought her off. 'I love you, Mikey,' she moaned, writhing in delight. I ground down on my own Michael, knowing that any second I'd be reacting in just the same way...

A little while afterwards Jennie and I were enjoying the dampness of our knickers as we began the long descent towards the green valley below. I caught the other Michael staring intently at my bum as it swayed from side to side beneath my skirt, and strangely I blushed with embarrassment, even though I'd felt no such embarrassment a few minutes earlier when he'd been studying it naked and on the job.

That fateful night we wined and dined far too well - for the second night in a row. Perhaps the product of the grape had something to do with what happened later. All four of us were well and truly blitzed by the time we'd staggered the short distance betwixt hostelry and hostel. As on the night before, Jennie and I slipped into bed and spent a delightful thirty minutes or so arousing each other in readiness for the trip along the corridor to visit our men. Then it was time for us to go and collect that to which we were legally entitled, and that for which we were more than ready.

The fine weather had broken and a storm was raging outside as we dressed in skimpy knickers and bras, and just then there was a terrifying crash of thunder and all the lights went out.

'Oh grief!' Jennie groaned. 'I can't see a thing. And the boys will be waiting for us.'

'We can feel our way to their room,' I said confidently. 'It's the second door on the right past the bathroom.'

Surprisingly our spouses were both fast asleep. We could hear them snoring softly as Jennie closed the bedroom door behind us. Too much beer, I reflected.

Carefully we groped our way forward in the dark until we located their beds, and before I had a chance to take further stock of the situation Jennie leapt enthusiastically on top of her unsuspecting husband and started on him, so I knelt on the floor beside my Michael, peeling back the sheets before running both hands over his naked stomach and groin. Even in his alcohol-enhanced sleep I could feel him begin to stiffen and stir. 'Mmm...' he sighed as he started to wake.

'I'm hungry,' I giggled naughtily, taking him deep into my mouth. He tasted beautiful, as always.

Jennie hadn't wasted any time either, and quickly I could hear the other bed starting to creak rhythmically. 'Oh!' she suddenly squealed in surprise, as the creaking suddenly quadrupled in pace. I blinked and tried to clear the booze from my brain. Something wasn't quite right, I can remember thinking to myself. But for the life of me I couldn't imagine what it was, so I gave up trying and concentrated on the matter in hand. Or rather, the matter in mouth...

Suddenly Michael came to the boil, spraying my lips and chin before I was able to direct his offering down my throat. I swallowed greedily, relishing the hot, salty taste. I kept him in my mouth even after he was fully spent, knowing I'd be able to revive him quite quickly that way. And sure enough, his sticky tip began to respond almost at once to the sort of resuscitation I always love to provide. I wriggled out of my skimpy knickers and slipped eagerly into my husband's bed.

Now both mattresses were creaking in unison as two girlie bottoms bounced rapidly up and down. Another flood of warm, sticky seed followed, making me spasm, and judging by the grunting and groaning beside me, both Jennie and her Michael were also in the throes of a really strong climax.

Michael kissed me; a long, passionate kiss that reminded me how much I loved him. I lay beneath his lean body, feeling my erect nipples boring into his chest. His penis had stopped contracting, resting comfortably inside me, still semi-erect. His hands were cupped under the cheeks of my bottom and I was delighted to feel him push a fingertip inside. And still the kiss continued, as passionate as ever. And as I wriggled my hips against his invading finger I could feel him starting to swell again. Soon he was fully rampant. Soon he was rigidly to attention inside me, ready to stretch me some more.

Away we went again, harder and faster than ever, and I could tell that the other two were following our excellent example. Jennie started squealing, her hands cupped over her mouth to smother the sound, and momentarily I was again struck by the thought that something was ever so slightly amiss. But I forgot it in seconds, due to the way Michael was shafting me so severely. I held my breath and concentrated every cell in my body on the way I was being so fearsomely fucked.

At last he began to explode once more, almost as hotly and copiously as before, stream after stream of his lovely thick sperm gushing into my womb and bringing me off with ease.

Eventually all four of us lay exhausted and still. Heavily laboured breathing was the only sound heard in the dark, then suddenly the electricity supply was restored and the lights came on. I blinked and looked up and around, and at that moment the truth - the whole terrible truth - dawned...

I stared in horror at my husband, a few feet to my side. I stared at him as he lay there, sprawled out and panting on top of a flush-faced Jennie. And he stared back at me as I lay naked under the other Michael. Now I understood the uneasy feeling I'd had earlier.

'Oh dear,' I gasped, 'I think there's been a bit of a mistake...'

And that's all there is to tell you, really. That's why Jennie and I are standing here facing the corner, our buttocks ablaze. That's why we're standing in front of our men, while they stare menacingly at our sore cheeks, cupped gingerly in hands that strive to soothe and console...

Chapter Nine - Alison Chairs the Board

Hi, it's Alison again. Now here's some worthwhile advice. This is for all you respectably married young ladies who find yourselves unexpectedly out of work. Don't, under any circumstances whatsoever, accept a temporary job working for the company where your husband has just been appointed personal assistant to the managing director. This is particularly true when the term of your employment is liable to span the Christmas festivities.

I'd been between jobs, following the sudden collapse of a not so small company, for 'cash flow' reasons. So I'd been kicking my heels at home for three weeks when Michael returned one evening with the news that there was a short-term vacancy in the word processing department of his firm. Cover was needed for someone on maternity leave.

'But I'm a sales executive,' I pointed out.

He retorted that I didn't appear to be selling very much at that particular moment, which was true, so I said I'd take the job. It would be easy enough to brush up on the typing skills I'd not used for nearly three years, I decided, and the money would be handy with Christmas just over a month away. And it would also be nice to see something of Michael during the course of the working day. My office would be on his floor, he informed me.

'Now you'll be able to keep a watchful eye on me,' I told him saucily, but lived to regret that remark.

Michael had only recently been appointed to his post as the managing director's right hand man. It was quite a feather in his cap, as well as a considerably increased monthly credit into his bank account, so on the strength of the promotion we'd moved house and more than doubled our mortgage.

But he had to watch his back. The MD was renowned for firing people for very little reason at all. Indeed, Michael's predecessor had been given the boot for something pretty trivial.

So as I said, Michael had to be very careful indeed, and I had to be careful too, for Michael's sake. I knew that Sir Roland - the managing director, known to his staff as Sir Rodent - would be quite prepared to visit any perceived sin of mine upon my hardworking husband. And as I said, we'd spent far more on the new house than we should have done, almost trebling our mortgage as well as running all our credit cards up to the maximum. So it was vital that neither of us did anything to jeopardise Michael's position...

It was the day before we stopped work for Christmas. The Christmas lunch in the executive dining room was a fairly boozy affair. Sir Roland had been happy to waive the no alcohol directive for the occasion, so consequently the wine flowed like water and everyone had a really good time.

Matters were improved further when Sir Roland announced that he had to leave early as he had an all-afternoon meeting with the chairman of the company's merchant bank. More bottles were opened and quickly emptied before it was time to return to our posts and allow the second sitting to make equally merry.

Michael was following me along the corridor that led to my department, so there we were alone, returning to work after the firm's Christmas lunch, Michael gazing, I'm sure, at the lateral swing of my buttocks beneath my smart black skirt.

'Very cheeky, Mrs North,' he growled, clapping a hand round my undulating right cheek and squeezing rather more forcefully than I'd expected. 'Very, very cheeky indeed.'

Immediately I could feel the crotch of my tight little knickers becoming damper as I smiled back at him over my shoulder. I turned to him, playfully squeezing the front of his trousers. As I'd expected he was already hard. Alcohol, plus the feel of my bottom, had woven a spell. Not that he needs alcohol to get that way, of course, but it does tend to make him that bit more dare-devilish, I suppose. And me as well, I have to admit. Without all that wine we'd had at lunchtime, we'd never have done what we subsequently did.

'I'm as horny as hell,' he breathed, both of his hands now locked round my bottom.

'I can feel,' I giggled naughtily, squeezing him again through his trousers. 'How about you?'

I squeezed my thighs together, already knowing the answer. 'I'm the same as you.'

'Let's fuck?' he croaked hoarsely. 'It's Christmas, and we are married, after all.'

Of course I should never have agreed to his very indecent proposal. Not on company premises, I mean to say. Not with the sort of brigand for whom we were working, absent or not. But my poor pussy was on fire. It demanded instant attention, my knickers becoming wetter and wetter. And as he said, we were married when all was said and done. It would be fun. It would be exciting to have a quickie with Michael at the office. Exciting and naughty, just like the old days. Exciting and naughty, but without any element of infidelity. The best of both worlds, I said to myself as we climbed the stairs that led to the top floor of the building. Michael slipped a hand up the back of my skirt, between my thighs and above my stockings.

'Jeez, you're wet,' he murmured appreciatively, pressing his fingers against the crotch of my panties.

'I'll be a great deal wetter when you're through with me,' I pointed out, but unfortunately this was to prove a not entirely accurate remark.

The boardroom was lit but deserted, as was the rest of the top floor, all of which was strictly out of bounds for both of us. The chairman and the finance director were abroad on holiday, and as I've already said, the feared MD was out on an appointment for the rest of the afternoon. So we felt safe enough.

As I walked towards the head of the huge oak table, just ahead of Michael, I hoisted my skirt up to my waist, saucily revealing pink panties and suspender belt, and there was a momentary stab of guilty conscience when I realised it was the same set I'd worn the previous Christmas for George's sake.

The table was large and set with writing pads, pencils and pens, and twenty leather-bound chairs stood guard around it. Michael gazed with evident approval at the sight of my scantily knickered bottom wiggling sexily from side to side, and when we were at the head of the table I pulled out one of the chairs and sat down.

'That's Sir Rodent's,' he warned.

'But he's not here.'

Michael knelt on the plush red carpet in front of me, struggling to undo his bulging zip. 'All the same,' he murmured nervously, 'I mean to say, you know, shagging on the Tyrant's own chair...'

I slid my panties down until they were dangling decoratively around my left ankle. 'In that case I'll make sure I give it a good wipe before we leave.'

Less than thirty seconds later Michael was between my parted, silk-stockinged legs, his lovely dick gliding sweetly in and out of my welcoming channel. 'That's nice,' I purred happily, as he pushed into me as far as he could go. 'Keep doing it just like that...'

I wrapped my legs tightly around him and then thrust hard against the power of his movement, and felt my juices seeping down between the cheeks of my bottom. The chair really would need a good wipe, I thought to myself, as he continued to fuck me with long, steady strokes that made my insides churn with delight. I closed my eyes and concentrated on the way I was being seen-to so effectively. Each slow insertion seemed longer and stronger than the previous one. How much I loved him, and how easily he could turn me on.

'Ohhh,' I moaned, taking a deep breath and grinding my bum from side to side 'Oh, Mike, that's so good. You're making me come...'

He slid both hands underneath my bottom and squeezed me firmly, at the same time stabbing forcefully against the neck of my womb and then resting there, bulky and hot, filling me to the brim. 'You're a very sexy lady, Mrs North,' he growled in my ear.

'Ohhh,' I moaned again, only louder, just as he started to move again. 'Oh yes, just like that. Long and slow like that.'

Suddenly there came a footfall in the corridor just outside the boardroom door, followed by a cough and a clearing of throat that was all too familiar to anyone who worked at that particular establishment. The MD, the Tyrant Rat, Sir Rodent, otherwise Sir Roland Rayke himself, was about to enter the boardroom where Michael and I were fucking like stoats! Fucking on his chair at the head of the boardroom table, for extra measure!

Even before the door handle started to turn Michael and I parted, leaving me disappointingly empty and alone, experiencing nothing but a longing ache where a moment earlier Michael's brawn had been.

'Get under the table,' I hissed in alarm, frantically pulling my skirt down as best I could. Michael obeyed in a flash, but as I was about to follow him the door swept open and Sir Roland stood framed in the doorway, looking straight at me.

'Hello,' he said, closing the door behind him and then moving closer to where I sat, blushing furiously. 'It's Alison, isn't it? Michael's wife?'

He was a distinguished man in his late fifties, with silver-grey hair and features that hinted at more than a degree of virility, and rumour had it that these looks were not in the least bit deceptive. His lady-killing exploits were well known amongst his employees.

'Er yes, Sir Roland,' I meekly gasped, surreptitiously tugging at the hem of my skirt until it reached the lacy pink tops of my stockings. Unfortunately the seat was still failing to cover most of my bum, but I didn't think it would be too obvious. After all, I was sitting firmly on the area in question.

'Are you waiting for someone?' he asked, as he stood in front of me.

'Oh, well, um yes, I am, Sir Roden... I mean, Sir Roland. Yes I am, actually...'

I followed his eyes as they travelled slowly but inexorably down to my feet. And then I groaned in despair, suddenly knowing exactly what he would spy.

'I see,' he mused thoughtfully. 'You're waiting here for someone, with a truly delightful little pair of pink knickers dangling so charmingly round your left foot. Is that correct?'

I opened my mouth to reply, but simply couldn't utter a word. Which was just as well, I suppose. I mean, whatever word could I possibly have uttered? I'd been caught fair and square. Caught in the act, red-faced and red-handed. Of explanation there was none.

'Could I enquire exactly whom you are awaiting?'

'Oh, well, erm...'

'Well, my dear, since you're waiting here in my boardroom and on my very own chair, I think I can only assume that you're waiting for me. Waiting for me, minus your pretty little knickers?' There was a very distinct glint in his eye as he spoke. A distinctly lecherous glint, to be precise. 'Am I right, my dear?' he asked smoothly, starting to unbuckle his belt.

I stared up at him in horror, still unable to reply.

'I think I can safely take your silence as confirmation,' he mused. 'Otherwise you would most certainly have disappointed me.' He was, of course, quite unaware of my husband out of sight under the table behind him as he slid his trouser zip down. At least, so I assumed at the time.

Next moment he was kneeling in Michael's former position between my thighs, his impressive erection spearing up in front of his white shirt and silk tie. I gulped and tried unsuccessfully to avert my eyes as he reached forward to lift the hem of my skirt above the shaven pink lips that lay wetly and warmly beneath.

'Very pretty,' he breathed avidly, gazing down at the glistening lips from which Michael had only just disengaged. 'And very ready for me, too.'

That was the moment of truth, the vital moment, the point of no return, the point at which either Michael or I had to pluck up enough courage to protest. Unfortunately both of us froze. I left it to him, and he left it to me - a somewhat fatal combination of hesitancy and doubt.

Then, before I could gather my wits, it was too late. Sir Roland thrust forward with deadly precision and, because of my condition of readiness, penetrated me fully and utterly.

'Ohhh,' I gasped, as I looked over his shoulder and saw Michael peering anxiously out at me from under the table. I stared back at him, hapless and helpless, full of another man's cock as we gazed at each other with startled eyes. *Stay there* I mouthed at him silently, just as his boss began to fuck me.

And didn't he just fuck me! Heavy strokes that filled me with rigid, pulsing flesh. Long, awesomely powerful strokes that seemed to take my breath away. I tried to keep silent, but very quickly my gasps turned to moans, and then the moans to groans of delight. I opened my eyes and was pleased to see that poor Michael had retreated out of sight. But I knew he could hear what was happening to me. I knew he could hear the squelching sound of Sir Roland thrusting in and out of me at speed... as well as my rapturous responses. Unfortunately there was nothing I could do to relieve Michael's plight. How awful he must be feeling, I thought, quite unable to prevent myself thrusting back with my hips and squealing with pleasure.

Wildly and noisily I began to orgasm, rolling my head from side to side and clutching the man tightly. Even though I knew my husband was witnessing it all I simply couldn't help myself. I simply couldn't control how my body was reacting to the vigorous assault.

When my climax was finally over he rested. I knew perspiration and tears were glistening on my cheeks as I opened my eyes and stared at my tormentor, perceiving at once the smug look of intense satisfaction on his face. 'You seemed to enjoy yourself a bit there,' he observed with a knowing smirk. 'Do you always come that much?'

'Yes, always,' I somehow managed to whisper, not entirely truthfully, more for Michael's sake, really.

But it was by no means finished yet. He withdrew, very wetly, and then helped me to my feet. 'I've spent the last six weeks admiring that sweet little bottom meandering its way around the building,' he informed me. 'It's far too pretty to keep hidden away on my chair. Let's treat ourselves. Let's have you on the floor on elbows and knees.'

I did as he ordered, skirt around my waist, forehead on the carpet, making sure that my bare bottom was angled back at the table in order to minimise the risk of Michael being discovered lurking underneath. Sir Roland settled heavily on top of me, his knees either side of mine, and his demanding dick pressed hard against the cheekiest part of my upturned buttocks.

Away he went again, screwing me from behind for all he was worth. In my new position - head down and bottom raised, like a supplicant before a sultan - he felt even bigger than before. So, gripping me tightly round the waist, he proceeded to slap his groin harder and harder into my uptilted cheeks, poking me really deeply. Now I knew that Michael was able to watch as well as hear the way I was being so extensively seen to. I knew he'd be able to see the other man's erection ploughing in and out. And did that thought give me some sort of twisted thrill? Well, all I can tell you is that I'd never known such a mixture of emotions; another orgasm building inside me while my husband knelt under the table, able to see for himself exactly how his boss was screwing me so prodigiously, and listening to me squealing with pleasure as well. I was ashamed at my own immodesty, of course, yet hugely aroused by the situation, the highly unconventional circumstances of the fuck seeming to add to the pleasure I cannot deny I felt...

A few seconds later there was even more of me on show to Michael, as Sir Roland pulled up my top and then unclipped my bra, allowing my breasts to tumble plentifully into the palms of his cupped hands. He massaged them with great enthusiasm, before eventually returning to his hold on my waist, thus allowing my breasts to swing back and forth in time with each powerful thrust. I supposed that Michael would notice how painfully erect my nipples had become, but it was something quite beyond my control. As was the way I gasped and moaned and groaned with pleasure. I was totally incapable of concealing how I felt.

On and on he screwed me, seeming never to tire. On and on at a fearsome pace, stretching me with every forward stroke. I could sense both men gazing intently at the exposed cheeks of my bottom, between which Sir Roland's gleaming cock was working briskly back and forth. Both of them, I just knew, were staring in fascination at the spectacle I made as I knelt, my forehead and elbows on the floor, my smoothly rounded buttocks offered up to Sir Roland for him to use howsoever he pleased.

After a while I judged he was approaching the end of the road. His grip on my waist was tighter than ever, and there was an intensity about the way he was pounding into me. So I risked twisting my head and looking back, and there was Michael, on all fours under the table, staring straight back at me with an expression I couldn't quite gauge. I widened my eyes at him, trying to convey the message that this wasn't any of my seeking, but I didn't dare look at him for too long, in case Sir Roland should wonder what I was doing and follow the direction of my gaze.

So I returned my forehead to the carpet and tried to forget about Michael and concentrate instead on the penis probing me so urgently from behind. I ground my hips and gasped again at the power I could feel in that demanding erection.

At long last I heard a choking grunt of contentment, and then felt him begin to empty himself into me. Stream after powerful stream, making me climax yet again. A shuddering climax accompanied by squeals of pure delight, and concerns that my obvious pleasure would make Michael feel awful.

'My dear girl,' croaked Sir Roland, his penis beginning to wilt at long last, 'please accept this as a mark of approval for the way this beautifully shaped bottom has so brightened the office in recent weeks.'

'Th... thank you, sir,' I mumbled, exhausted, overwhelmed by the ferocity of my orgasm.

Sir Roland stood up, leaving me kneeling on the carpet, bare-breasted, bare-bottomed, and already starting to leak his seed. He tucked himself back into his underpants and trousers and then helped me up.

'Thank you,' I murmured breathlessly, more than a trifle unsteady on my feet

'Now then, my dear,' he said with an unexpected degree of frostiness in his voice, 'I don't know which of your male, or for that matter, female, acquaintances is skulking under the table, and I don't particularly want to know, bearing in mind it's Christmas and I'm feeling charitable. But I do believe that I need to reinforce the point that this boardroom is strictly for the use of the company's directors, and no one else. I think I need to make that abundantly clear to you.'

'Yes, Sir Roland,' I said weakly as he sat on the chair next to his own and purposefully patted his lap.

'Settle yourself over my knee, young lady, leaving your knickers where they are around your ankle, of course. I want to make absolutely sure the lesson is well and truly learnt.'

I stared at him in confusion, assuming I must have misheard or misunderstood. Surely he wasn't meaning to do what I thought... 'I beg your pardon, Sir Roland?' I gulped.

'Over my knee, young lady,' he repeated. 'You have to learn that company rules exist to be obeyed.'

Blushing furiously, I folded myself across his lap as demurely as circumstances would permit, my bare bottom tipped saucily up at him and very much at his mercy. I could feel his eyes devouring my buttocks as I lay there, nervously awaiting my fate. How much did he intend to hurt me? More than George last Christmas? More than Michael on holiday in Cumbria? Knowing Sir Roland I couldn't imagine he was going to be gentle with me. How humiliating it was, lying there while he measured me up for the punishment ahead, and took all the time in the world to savour the situation.

At last he spoke, and I knew the worst. My fears were fully confirmed. 'Personally, my dear, I think the diligent application of my hand, followed by my belt, will be more than sufficient to act as a cogent reminder in future.'

Sir Roland was to be proved entirely correct. By the time I was allowed to regain my feet my poor backside was blazing with an intensity I'd never thought possible. Would it ever be the same again? The belt had seared me so deeply that I felt sure its mark would remain with me forever. He'd known exactly what he was doing, I'm sure. He'd known exactly how to cause maximum suffering. My right cheek had been subjected to the hardness of his hand for a good five minutes, followed by the left. Then the belt was utilised in the same manner, time after time, raising one blotchy swelling after another. And finally his hand was used again, this time to emphasise to me the extent of the hurt the belt had inflicted. I tried my best not to sob too pitifully, for Michael's sake, but it was simply impossible to undergo that sort of ordeal in silence. It was the most painful punishment I've ever endured.

He got up and stood behind me. I glanced back over my shoulder, trying to blink back tears, and saw that he was staring down at my burning buttocks with obvious relish. 'Yes, Mrs North,' he said smoothly, sounding well pleased with himself, 'I think I can safely assure the rest of my board that here at least is one temporary employee who has now learnt the importance of paying much stricter attention to company rules and regulations. Would you feel able to agree with me there?'

I ran my hands over my injured parts, very tentatively. 'Yes, Sir Roland,' I muttered ruefully, 'I seem to have learnt it very thoroughly indeed.' And learnt it I certainly had. I never took the slightest liberty with Sir Roland again.

'Good. And hopefully whoever is still concealing himself, or herself, under the table will also take that point onboard. I shall not be so generous again.

'Merry Christmas, young lady,' he continued, 'even if you do have to spend much of it on your feet.'

The door closed behind Sir Roland and I heard Michael crawling out from under the table behind me. But I didn't dare look at him; never had I been in a sorrier state for my husband to see. There I stood, comprehensively fucked and punished by our mutual employer, and with all essential items of clothing where they shouldn't be. Hurriedly I began to make myself decent, pulling up knickers and fastening bra, before turning to look him in the eye... and blushing deeply once more. 'I'm sorry,' I said unhappily, pulling down my top, 'but what else could I have done?'

He smiled rather wanly, but his eyes were full of the love I know he feels for me. 'Nothing,' he said softly. 'I should have done or said something.'

'But you couldn't, any more than I could,' I comforted him. I realised my skirt was still around my waist and pulled it down, wincing as it brushed over my beaten bum. 'Are you okay?' I asked anxiously. 'It must have been awful for you. How did you feel, stuck under the table while he... um... you know?'

'Very jealous,' he admitted, 'and frustrated. But proud of you, too.'

'I'll make it up to you tonight,' I whispered, still red in the face. 'And there is one consolation,' I added, 'about what's just happened, I mean.'

'Oh,' he said, 'and what's that?'

I smiled at him mischievously. 'Our job prospect's have never been better.'

Chapter Ten - Alison's Anguish

Here's another painful confession about how accidents just seem to dog me. This time I blame the GIGO principle for yet another tumble from my would-be state of grace.

The principle that says that when you work with computers, garbage in equals garbage out. I'm not referring to my own PC, of course. No items of garbage have ever been allowed to infiltrate that very high-tech piece of equipment. My boss, the director of sales, would have been most displeased had I ever allowed that to happen. No, I'm referring to the ancient piece of junk that the modelling/theatrical agency laughingly refers to as its 'fully computerised system for matching models/actresses with suitable job opportunities'.

You see, although my salary as the sales director's PA was very good, I was topping it up with a few quick photo or video shoots for the advertising industry; lingerie commercials and that sort of thing. Well, to be honest, lingerie commercials full stop. It seemed the only role for which I was suited was that of a young lady wearing just the skimpiest attire possible. I can't begin to think why...

'Look, Sylvia,' I said into the phone one day, to the agency's managing director, 'are you sure your computer's got me down for anything other than naughty knickers and bras?'

'Yes, of course it has,' she replied.

'Well, it only seems to match me with those sort of assignments. You're sure it's properly up to the job?'

'Yes, it's very, er, reliable indeed.' She sounded a trifle unsure, but at the time no alarm bells rang in my head... unfortunately.

'How new is it?' I asked.

'Not particularly new, but it has been upgraded... sort of...'

'I know you've got several hundred girls on your books,' I continued. 'If it's not state-of-the-art, do you think it could have gone a bit wobbly when it comes to my file?'

'I'm sure it hasn't. But what I'll do is check your profile myself and rewrite it if necessary. How's that?'

'Thanks, Sylvia, that'll be fine. I'll look forward to receiving something a little bit different next time.'

'I'm sure you'll get it, Alison.'

And so I did. But not quite in the manner she meant...

Three days later the short script arrived - for a knicker commercial! The model is topless, although her hands are discreetly covering her breasts, and she's lying back on a huge waterbed, rather blatantly displaying her most recent purchase to her husband. He rushes over to the bed but grabs the telephone, not the model, much to her obvious disgust. But surprise, surprise, urgently he rings his credit card company and implores them to double his wife's credit limit. Then he makes a dive for her... end of advertisement.

It would probably never be shown, I thought, but it could be broken down into a series of stills for newspapers and magazines. The fee income wouldn't be so great, but it would be better than none at all.

So much for Sylvia tweaking up my file on the agency's computer; I'd already done more than half a dozen shoots on an almost identical theme!

Next day a computer generated appointment card arrived in the post, together with a small packet containing the tiny pair of semi-transparent black knickers I was to wear for the filming.

Two days later another appointment card arrived, and without any explanation it gave me a different appointment at a different location. Obviously things had changed, so I threw the old card away and made a note in my diary of the new time and place for me to parade before the camera in just my lacy black undies.

By coincidence I bumped into Sylvia that evening, in a popular wine bar I occasionally frequent.

'Thanks for the new contract,' I said, with just a hint of sarcasm.

'I told you our computer was better than you thought,' she replied enigmatically, before leaving with some young blade who definitely wasn't her husband.

Better than I'd thought? Yet another knicker advert? Where was the variety of work in that? Where was the chance to model some make-up, or a really smart cocktail dress? Or the chance of a minor television role, come to that? After all, the agency catered for a wide range of work, not just modelling. And I had my union card.

'Sylvia's done her best for you,' confirmed her assistant, the pretty young lady still sitting at the bar sipping a glass of sparkling white wine. 'She spent ages tapping into your file to make sure we could match you with all sorts of different jobs. It's not her fault if the computer's a bit long in the tooth.'

Even then I felt no cause for alarm.

It was a dirty-white building, and on the front door there was a push-button with a speak-into/out-of box. 'Alison North,' I replied, when a remote voice asked for my name.

There came a buzz, followed by the crackle of, 'The door's unlocked. You're filming on the sixth floor.'

There was no lift, so I trooped up the staircase, telling myself that the exercise would do me good. *Omega Films*, read the name on the door, so I knocked and turned the handle.

'I'm Ken, the director,' said a middle-aged man with thinning long hair, stripping me with his eyes and making my insides flip a little, 'and aren't you just perfect for the part...'

'Thank you,' I murmured, looking around the room. Yes, there by the window was the bed. Not actually a waterbed, but large and comfortable and with black satin sheets pulled down to the foot. Two professional cameras were angled at it, one from either side. 'Hi,' I said to the two cameramen grinning at me.

'Hi,' they mumbled together.

I turned back to Ken. 'I've studied the script quite closely,' I told him, knowing he'd approve. 'And I must say how enthusiastic I am about it.' It does no harm, I've discovered, to suck up to those in positions of influence.

But he looked rather puzzled. 'We're off-script today,' he replied with a frown.

'Off-script?'

'Yes, that's right. It's more convincing to improvise, you know.'

'Oh,' was all I could say.

'Would you get undressed, please,' he said, nodding at a screen in the corner of the room. 'Behind there, if you prefer. We're a bit behind schedule, I'm afraid.'

'Where's my husband?' I asked, moving to the screen, which had a wooden chair behind it. I was referring to my screen hubby, of course.

'He'll enter when I cue him. We're going straight into filming. No rehearsals. No time, I'm sorry to say.'

I peeled off my clothes except for the filmy black knickers that had arrived through the post. Clearly they'd changed a lot of the proposed commercial. According to my script the first scene was the husband standing at the foot of the bed admiring the way in which the wife was turning her hips in order to show him both the front and rear of the recently purchased panties.

I walked out from behind the screen, fingertips demurely shielding my nipples. Ken glanced down at the tiny triangle of silk stretched across my sex mound, tight between my thighs.

'Good improvising,' he said approvingly, making me wonder just what he meant. I asked, but he didn't answer, instead walking behind me. I could sense his gaze all over my bottom. 'Very nice,' he muttered, almost to himself. 'In fact, just what the director ordered.'

I opened my mouth to respond, but was at a loss to murmur more than, 'Thanks.'

The lighting was turned on and I was gestured to the floodlit bed. 'Just spread yourself out, love,' directed Ken. 'On your front, and give this camera a really sexy sideways look... yep, that's great. Hold it just like that... okay, here we go...'

So I gazed into the camera with the most sultry expression I could manage, and as I did so the second camera worked slowly up and down my body, pausing to dwell lingeringly on my scarcely covered buttocks.

'That's great. Keep moving your bum slowly and sexily, just like that,' directed Ken, and I did exactly as he said, one camera panning in on my face and the other on the seat of my filmy knickers.

'Enter the husband!' Ken called; a door opened and in strode one of the biggest hunks I've ever seen in my life. Muscles rippled through his tight T-shirt and jeans, and immediately I started to moisten at the sight of him - an automatic reaction over which I had no control. One camera stayed on me, the other moved to him. Discretely I squeezed my thighs together and savoured the sensation in the pit of my tummy.

'Caught you,' he growled, glaring angrily down at me. 'Caught you right in the act!'

'What the...?' I gasped in amazement.

'I was waiting outside in the phone box,' he went on. 'I was waiting there when John came out of the house no more than sixty seconds ago. Caught you right in the act, you cheating little strumpet!'

'I don't know what you're talking about!' I wailed in despair.

'Don't give me that!' he snarled, looming over the bed with considerable menace, followed by camera one. 'I've told you; I was waiting outside in the street. I was expecting something like this, after the way you've been behaving towards him. Particularly the way you threw yourself at him last night.'

'Hey,' I gasped in alarm as he clamped two large hands on my shoulders, ensuring I remained on my front, 'what's going on here?'

'I'll show you what's going on. I'll show you what happens to a randy young housewife who's just fucked her husband's best mate!' So saying he began to force my arms behind my back.

'Stop that!' I shrieked, struggling hopelessly. 'Leave me alone! What do you think you're doing?'

'That's it,' enthused Ken, giving me the thumbs-up sign. 'That's the ticket. Fight as hard as you can, girl.'

I didn't need any directing to do that with great realism, but it was all to no avail. My 'husband' was pinning me facedown on the bed, one hand gripping my wrists behind my back while his other tugged my skimpy black knickers unceremoniously down to my knees. 'Stop that,' I wailed, trying desperately to free my hands and roll over onto my back.

But it was no use at all. However much I struggled and protested I was held as securely as if I'd been bound in chains. 'What do you think you're doing?' I asked over my shoulder. He was now sitting on the bed, holding me down with one muscle-bound arm. He had a leg across both of mine, ensuring they stayed flat on the bed. Then he stuffed one of the pillows under my hips so my bottom was raised and vulnerable.

'I've already told you,' he said, raising his free hand. 'This is what your arse can expect for what you've just done with John.'

'I didn't do anything!' I protested, confused.

Splat! His hand landed heavily on the fleshiest part of my left buttock.

'Ouch!' I howled, jerking my head back as I did so. 'Ouch!' I howled again as he repeated the treatment with all his force. 'Ouch!' I howled again, and again, tears meandering down my cheeks while camera two captured the image of my grief-stricken face - and while camera one was no doubt focussed on my sorely abused bum.

After what seemed ages, he changed tactics and began to attack the other defenceless buttock. On and on he spanked, scalding it to the same degree he had its twin. I yelped and struggled and kicked, but the stinging smacks continued to rain down without relenting.

'I'm the wrong girl,' I tried to sob - but could only manage a feebly mumbled protest.

Of course I knew exactly what had happened. Sylvia had been tweaking my file on her ancient computer, with the result that its out of date metal insides had cancelled my first contract, and instead sent me on an assignment to take part in a spanking movie! I knew already that the agency went in for some of the seamier aspects of the entertainment industry. I knew that from some of the questions Sylvia had asked me when she originally opened my file; even though I'd told her I was definitely not interested in making a sex film.

'That's it, you two,' Ken cut in at long last, and thankfully the beating stopped.

My assailant moved from the bed, leaving me lying face down. I could hear the rustle of rapidly discarded clothing and wearily turned my head to peer at him. My 'husband' was as naked and erect as any young 'wife' could possibly want. I gazed in fascination at the sturdy appendage that reared so rampantly towards his belly button. I tried to be ladylike and look away, but the sight was just too intriguing, and in the pit of my stomach something too familiar started to stir...

'Focus on his dick,' Ken instructed camera one. 'I want a really long shot of that brute before the action begins. And you, camera two, give me a shot of her face as she stares at it. And Alison, that's good, keep on looking every bit as hungry for it as that. Good... excellent... yes, lick your lips again.'

And so I finally knew the worst. I was at last aware of the whole horrifying truth. It wasn't just a spanking video in which I'd become so unwittingly embroiled; it was a full-scale, hardcore movie! Starring innocent little me!

So what do you think happened next? Did I struggle to my feet, hands gingerly nursing my bright red bottom, and advise Ken and company of the computer's ghastly mistake?

Did I explain exactly how I'd originally thought I'd be filming a legitimate knicker commercial, and then beat a hasty retreat?

Did I just lie there on the bed, exhausted, shocked, but shamefully turned on, waiting for the male model to fuck me?

Did I just lie there, facedown, pushing my sorely spanked bottom back against his groin until he filled me with his seed?

Did I just lie there for twenty minutes or so, being screwed by a bloke whose name I didn't know while Ken directed the cameramen to get detailed close-ups of the whole lurid performance...?

And what did I say to Michael when I finally got home that night? Did I keep my blistered backside safely under wraps for several days, an almost impossible task, or did I tell him the truth? The truth about the accidental spanking, I mean.

The truth about the way in which Sylvia's old computer had sent me on entirely the wrong job. Not the truth about the truly unbelievable fuck that may - cr may not - have followed...

    After all, I was under contract, wasn't I?